This Nervous
   Is Driving

This Nervous Breakdown Is Driving Me Crazy

A Collection of Short Stories

by Annie Reiner

DOVE
BOOKS

ISBN 0-7871-0707-7

Printed in the United States of America

Dove Books
8955 Beverly Boulevard
West Hollywood, CA 90048

Distributed by Penguin USA

Text design and layout by Carolyn Wendt
Jacket design and layout by Anne-Marie Dalton
Jacket illustration by Annie Reiner

First Printing: July 1996

10 9 8 7 6 5 4 3 2 1

Contents

Acknowledgments

The poem in "The White River Scroll" was first published in *Mind Your Head* by Annie Reiner, Wilshire House, Los Angeles, 1991.

Special thanks to Charlotte Gusay, for her faith in my work, and to Lorraine Rose for her uncommon wisdom.

To My Parents

With gratitude for their enormous
love and support . . .
and for driving me crazy.

A Special
Morning Report

If a man die
it is because death
has first
possessed his imagination.
　　—*William Carlos Williams*

Sam Daniels rolled out of
bed and faced the cameras with droopy eyes. He
opened the paper at breakfast, and there under the
headline he read: "Sam Daniels awoke with hope this
morning, despite the weight of encroaching years."
Sam shrugged, but his lips quivered into a slight grin
as he read on.

"Obviously revivified by a night of bliss, his face
in the mirror—now freshly shaved—revealed few of
the deep crevices you would expect from a sixty-four-
year-old man."

"Sixty-three," Sam muttered.

The article went on to praise his choice of wardrobe this unseasonably warm spring morning—a beige suit with a pristine white shirt and peach-colored tie, taupe Italian shoes. He gulped down the last of his coffee, kissed his much younger wife good-bye, and got on his way.

The radio blasted at him, rap music that replayed in his head the roar of gunfire from the war. But this was a new invasion, of a society he no longer recognized. He turned quickly to the K-NOB news.

"Sam Daniels almost got indigestion today from his hastily gobbled breakfast, lovingly prepared by his pretty wife, who is half his age. As if Fran Daniels doesn't have enough on her mind with her own landscaping business, she awoke this morning before dawn to make Sam his favorite: French toast."

"That's not my favorite," Sam said quietly.

"Fran is certainly one beautiful, talented woman. We hope Sam Daniels knows how lucky he is."

"Believe me, I know," he mumbled. He smiled at the thought of her, but his pleasure was short-lived. After a series of annoying little beeps, a news flash came over the airwaves. "This is Tom Bailey with a K-N-O-B special morning report. Sam Daniels has an eleven o'clock meeting this morning, about which he has completely forgotten. I repeat, Sam Daniels of Wyler and Daniels Law Offices, Inc., is scheduled to meet with Mr. Roosevelt from Roosevelt and Roosevelt Textiles at eleven o'clock, and he forgot to write it down. We believe he scheduled something else for eleven-thirty but that is all the information we have at this time."

Sam couldn't believe his ears. Struggling to get his appointment book from his briefcase on the seat beside him, he swerved recklessly.

"Watch where you're going, asshole!" the driver next to him yelled as Sam sped away.

"Close call," the radio piped in, referring to the nearly missed appointment. Sam looked in his book under Monday at eleven o'clock and there it was— nothing. That proves nothing, he thought. Nothing written down was no proof at all that something was missing. He didn't recall having spoken with anyone from R and R Textiles.

"We know that it is not like Sam Daniels to make a mistake of this kind," the K-NOB special report continued, "but it's not unheard of these days, either. We feel it's too soon to assume any serious problem, say Alzheimer's disease or stroke or incipient senility.

No, at this juncture our best guess on this mysterious oversight is that Sam . . . well . . . he forgot. And that's our special morning report. Back to you, Jennifer."

"Thank you, Tom."

"Forgot?" Sam said. "Forgot?"

He parked his car and hurried through the lot, barely bothering to smile for the camera that greeted him as usual upon his arrival.

"Not now, fellas," he mumbled, but one newsman managed to corner him for a statement.

"Is it true you almost forgot an appointment today, Sam?" the man asked, sticking a microphone under his nose.

"No comment."

"Well then, tell me, how are things going for you today generally?"

"What a mess," Sam muttered to himself. "I don't know what's going on."

"You heard it here," the newscaster said to the camera as Sam hurried into the building. "Sam Daniels doesn't know what's going on."

His secretary, Lois, had no record of the appointment.

"I've been with you for twenty-seven years," she reassured him, "and I haven't once overlooked an appointment, have I?" Sam was somewhat relieved, but what about the morning report?

"There's always a first time," he said anxiously, and asked Lois to call Roosevelt and Roosevelt.

"Do you want Roosevelt or Roosevelt?" she asked, a critical question as it turned out, for Roosevelt *fils* was suing Roosevelt *père* and Sam had been asked to represent one of them in court. The question was, which one?

Minor upsets like these had been happening for months. If it hadn't been for those early morning news flashes and special reports on the evening news, Sam would probably have lost his practice by now. So far he had managed to keep these lapses hidden from almost everyone except Lois—even from the wife whom at his age he was indeed lucky to have.

Sam got home late that evening and as usual Fran greeted him with a smile and a hearty meal. He looked at her—she *was* pretty, but not as pretty as her pictures in the newspapers and magazines. In those she was always done up and shown at her best, her face lit by the sense of importance a camera bestows on someone who's being made into a public icon. At home she looked like a normal woman.

Sam sat down at his TV tray and switched on the

set while he waited for Fran to bring his dinner.

"How was your day, honey?" she asked as she dished out his roasted potatoes. "I hope the chicken came out the way you like it. Chicken Basquaise," she said, "your favorite."

That's not my favorite, he thought as he watched her walk back into the kitchen. Still, it smelled good. His eyes returned to the set and he saw Fran there, walking into the kitchen. She stirred a pot of peas and adjusted the flame under the chicken. Then, on second thought, she turned it off. He was comforted to see her busy in the kitchen, wiping down the counter and running water in the sink to soak the pots.

"Do you want some wine?" she asked, looking straight at the camera. Her face in closeup appeared flawless, and the gauze over the lens certainly never hurt.

"I'll have a little, sure. Thanks, dear," he answered, and he watched her go to the refrigerator to get a bottle of chardonnay. Her ass looked great as she bent over to where the wine lay on the bottom shelf. Sam took a bite of chicken and smiled.

Fran appeared beside him with the wine. After she'd set it down he took her hand and kissed it. She was like a goddess and he could hardly wait for her to return to the kitchen so he could get a long shot of her as she made a plate of food for herself.

She came back and sat down at her TV tray with her chicken. No potatoes—she was on a diet, though there wasn't an ounce of excess flesh on her.

"Let's keep it that way," she always said. "Anyway, you know the camera puts on five pounds."

The usual programming had resumed and Sam and Fran watched "Roseanne" between bites. They laughed at her brash, brazen comments. It was so earthy, so real.

After dinner they watched the first part of a new dramatic series called "Judgment in Paradise," about a normal law practice except it was in Hawaii. Then Sam watched Fran do the dishes. Bored with that, he switched to the local news. Anchorman George Willis praised Fran's Chicken Basquaise—"Sam's favorite," he said—but went on to add that her salad dressing had a little too much vinegar.

"You got *that* right," Sam said, but he was slightly dismayed at what seemed to be the conventional wisdom about the Chicken Basquaise. Her Chicken Dijon was much more to his liking, much more piquant. He was frustrated at being misrepresented with no way to communicate his true preference so he switched off the TV news and went back to Fran. She

7

was just finishing up the nasty baked-on crust of the potato pan and he longed to come up and put his arms around her waist, to kiss her neck and smell the soft scent of perfume in her hair. Then he switched to old reruns of "Burns and Allen."

He was worried about the Roosevelt case. Fran came up behind his easy chair and put her arms around him. She kissed his cheek, a scene he would have just loved to have seen recreated on screen, but the eleven o'clock news would soon be reporting the Dow Jones Industrial average.

"Good evening. Our top breaking story tonight is the dramatic rescue of little Eva Rehnquist of Oklahoma City from a raging fire in which she was trapped early this morning."

"Oh, isn't that wonderful!" Fran exclaimed. Of course it *was* wonderful, Sam realized, but he needed to know if his stocks were safe.

"Isn't she adorable?" Fran said. "God, her parents must be ecstatic."

"On the local scene," the news continued, "Sam Daniels is more interested in his own selfish financial concerns than in the life of an adorable three-year-old girl. Can you believe the depths to which humanity has sunk?"

Sam looked guiltily at Fran who was thumbing through *House Beautiful* and did not appear to have heard the scathing editorial.

"Yes, adorable," Sam agreed belatedly. "She's a lucky little girl, all right," he said with pathos.

"And everyone was so helpful, the neighbors and the firemen and all," Fran said. "It does one's heart good to see such selflessness."

"It sure does," Sam said sheepishly.

He flicked the remote control and the picture died in the set.

Fran, feeling amorous, cuddled up close to Sam when they got into bed. He had an early morning and was reluctant, but Fran knew just what got him going and before he knew it they were making love. He had never felt so passionate as he did with Fran, but lately he found himself wondering what it would look like tomorrow on "The Today Show." Maybe they won't even cover it this time, he'd tell himself, just so he could get on with the business at hand. But then he'd feel a surge of ecstasy so transcendent that he knew this would be big news. Surely one of the networks would carry it. Their sex life had gotten so wonderful he could no longer enjoy it, but he managed in spite of this to have an orgasm. Still, nothing fools the camera, and in the morning Jane Pauley revealed to the world the superior nature of their lovemaking. She then went on to add, "We might as well face it, though. Mr. Daniels is no spring chicken, and at his age, well, let's just say he brought things to a very 'respectable conclusion.'"

Head hung low, Sam switched off the TV and finished knotting his tie. Fran was as cheerful and sunny as ever and seemed not to have observed as much as Jane Pauley had. She embraced him lovingly and stroked his gray hair. No perfunctory peck on the cheek this morning—her kiss was informed by the previous night's passion and Sam became excited all over again. "At my age, at my age," he thought vengefully, the words ringing in his ears as he led his wife back upstairs. He would demand a retraction from the network and a personal apology from Jane Pauley. After all, it was her fault in the first place that he was distracted. If she would stop reporting every goddamn move he made, he might have gone on to fulfill the true promise of the evening.

Fran had to get to work early herself that day and seemed unable to get into the spirit. When she suggested they wait until evening, Sam was disappointed, but relieved, too, afraid perhaps to find out that Jane Pauley was right.

He rode to work in silence until he couldn't stand it anymore, and then he turned on K-NOB. It was the musical portion of their programming, thank God, and Sam listened peacefully as he drove up Lakeside Boulevard. The blue of the lake sparkled, and Sam felt young—or rather, ageless, as one does when one is young. Humming off-key, his mind wandered and he missed his turnoff.

"We interrupt with the following bulletin—"

"Now what?" Sam said, but then realizing his mistake, quickly doubled around and headed back on the Boulevard. Unfortunately, Tom Bailey of K-NOB just wouldn't leave it at that, and for the first time he used words like *senile* and *incompetent*.

"That's absurd!" Sam barked at the radio. He switched the station but it was no use. K-RAC was covering his mistake, too, as was K-SOL. He turned back to K-NOB which by now was well into last night's sexual encounter, going into more graphic detail than Jane Pauley ever could on television, citing specific acts as evidence of waning passion.

"Tragic, tragic encroachment of old age, which I regret in this case may mean that death itself is not far away."

"Oh, come on," Sam shouted. "That's ridiculous!

11

I never felt better in my life."

The radio laughed.

"You guys are exaggerating, check your sources. Exaggerating? Hell, these are outright lies. I'm fit as a fiddle, maybe a little distracted sometimes, but no one ever died of that."

"Well, it's all over," he heard Tom Bailey announce in solemn tones. "We tried to warn him, but some people just refuse to listen. A great man in his own small way: Sam Daniels, loving husband, adequate lawyer, tragically, dead at sixty-four years old."

"What?" Sam exploded. "What are you talking about? Sixty-*three*! I'm sixty-*three* years old, goddamn it! It's you who're getting senile, not me! You've done nothing but report errors for days now—errors and lies! First it was the French toast, and now death! It's an outrage! Is no one responsible for the information they spill into the airwaves anymore? Lies! Errors and lies, and I won't stand for it. I tell you, you won't get away with it this time!"

In his rage, Sam failed to notice the curve in the road. He failed to notice the cement wall growing larger and larger in front of him. By the time he did notice, it was too late. The car was crushed like an accordion and only by his driver's license and his teeth could they identify that it was indeed Sam Daniels who, at the age of sixty-three (or four), was tragically dead.

"We now resume our normal programming with a half hour of continuous music."

Married Lives

My husband came in wearing a fur hat and a full-length overcoat with a heavy woolen scarf wrapped tightly around his neck.

"It's sixty degrees out," I said with a quizzical look.

"I am Russky!" he bellowed in a phony Russian accent.

"Yes, darling, but you and I were both born here in New Jersey, and it's spring."

I should have known better by that time than to point out the obvious to Sergei, for when he decided to undertake a new personality it was useless to try to stop him. He attempted to answer me with a snappy Russian retort but was immediately faced with the fact that he does not speak a word of the language.

"But I *am* Russian, aren't I?" he whined, overcome with doubt. "Why do you do this to me?"

I came to expect these sudden identity changes after a while and to take the various facets of Sergei in my stride, but it was not always like this.

The first real hint that something was wrong occurred the week after we got married. That was Sergei's first transformation, and I remember my mother telling me that if I did not leave him right then and there, I was crazy, too. He's not crazy, I told her, and I think this is true, because since then every one of his personalities has always been at least loosely connected to his true self. I have always chosen to see it as variations on a theme rather than insanity. For instance, he *is* of Russian descent, and that first time on our honeymoon when he came in dressed like a mime I simply told myself that he was by nature a rather quiet fellow anyway. Never one of those boisterous men constantly trying to show you how much they know, Sergei was gentle, humble, quiet. So when he came in dressed like a mime, although I did not exactly understand his purpose or reason, I must admit it made a certain kind of sense. Love, in my case, was not blind, just a little confused.

Since we did not venture outside the honeymoon suite much anyway, what did it really matter if Sergei wanted to dress up like a mime? And why take offense at every one of life's little mysteries? In those days we said much more with our eyes than it is possible to say with words, so in that regard Sergei's complete and utter silence was barely worthy of note.

By the time we returned home I was used to him as a mime. I was even rather sorry to see him change back into his ordinary business suit, for it brought with it the dolorous impression that a magical phase of our relationship was over. How wrong I was.

It was very exciting in the early days. I never knew who would show up for dinner or who would be there to greet me when I came home. Sergei the Prince, Sergei the Risible Waiter, Sergei the Drunk. I never should have told my mother about that one, but she happened to call up right after the Drunk had left for work for the first time and it just slipped out. Amused, I said to her, "Guess what, Ma? Sergei's a drunk." She didn't laugh. She did not understand that it was merely another one of his incarnations, so her response was decidedly grim. I always said that Sergei should have married my mother, for as far as he was concerned she always responded correctly to the whole thing, while my reactions were usually a big disappointment to him. He relished his changes from one character to another and he claimed that my patient forbearance made it almost impossible for him to feel the difference.

"Play along, play along," he would tell me, exasperated at my good-natured laughter. "You think I go to all this trouble for nothing?"

I must say, he *had* gone to quite a bit of trouble for the Drunk—including losing his job—so naturally he expected that I would act like any normal wife and be upset.

"Come on, cry," he would badger, staggering around in front of me. "At least get angry!" he would scream as he picked up an ashtray and hurled it across the room. But I knew Sergei better than to think this drunken slob could be my husband, so it was hard to get upset.

"You'll get another job, honey. Don't worry," I said, managing to suppress a smile.

"I'm not worried. I want *you* to worry."

"When *you* worry," I told him, "then I'll worry. Until then, honey, enjoy yourself."

Because I was such a good sport, Sergei would invite my mother over to get angry. She more than made up for my laissez-faire, and he had a great time reeling around the room, abusing us both with his drunken remarks and being chastised to his heart's content. My mother never let him down. At first she would just glare at Sergei in silent disapproval, but all he had to do was utter one sloppy, obsequious, "Nice to see you, Mama," and she would take the bait, lighting into him with what a no-good, drunken bum he was, how he didn't deserve her daughter, and so on. I found the two of them very funny together so I laughed even more than usual, and this sent my mother through the roof, which in turn made Sergei even happier.

It wasn't always easy, however. One day I announced to my husband, "Darling, I'm pregnant!" How pleased I was as I looked lovingly into his eyes, scarcely believing that we had been blessed with this miracle.

"Oh, how wonderful," he smiled. "Who's the father?"

You see, that week he was a Folies Bergères girl, so he figured it couldn't have been he. I did not laugh at that one, but to my surprise, this time he was upset that I *didn't* laugh. With the carefree spirit of a Folies dancer he could hardly be expected to take seriously our blessed event. Relationships can be very complicated, I told myself.

"Play along, play along," he always coached. It

was a constant source of irritation to Sergei not to have it his way; and eventually the criticisms began to wear down my amiable nature.

"Why didn't you marry my mother?" I complained, since he obviously liked her reactions so much. I never should have given him the idea, because for the next full month he became my father. This I felt was asking too much of me and I told him so. But by being my father he was sure he could trick me into being my mother and finally playing along. I imagine that as far as Sergei was concerned he was only trying to improve our relationship, but the whole thing backfired. Although he did a masterful job of impersonating my father, in every other way it was a disaster. Our sex life all but disappeared. I just couldn't. And while Sergei expected to evoke my mother, he still got me—but a me he did not even recognize. In short, I regressed to some sort of pre-Oedipal level of development. This was more than he could take, and finally Sergei was forced to admit defeat.

I hoped that things would slowly get back to normal, but alas, it was not to be, and I began to fear that after having been my father some irrevocable change had taken place in Sergei. For an awfully long time my husband became plain old Sergei Geronovsky, and after several long months of this I began to yearn for the excitement of the early days. Would I ever see another pirate bounding down the stairs to greet me? Or even a pencil or a bowl of fruit, from the days when he favored inanimate objects?

Years passed—it is hard to believe—and every night he came home in his banker's three-piece suit and the polka-dot tie he was wearing the very first day I met him. He was certainly more serene, and I guess I should have been glad about that, but it wasn't long before I began to think that if I saw that polka-dot tie one more morning I might have to move out to avoid dying of boredom. I admit I once went so far as to convince him it was Saturday just so I wouldn't have to look at that tie.

I love my husband and I did not want to leave him, but I felt as if something were missing. What it was I could not exactly say, but every time I looked at that tie I saw the tangible evidence of something that wasn't there. Something had to be done. I bought him a new tie, very expensive and very beautiful, pure silk in a delicate print, muted shades of blue and gray to go with his gray suit.

"What's the occasion?" he asked as I handed him the box.

"Nothing special. It's just because I love you," I lied. What sweet relief I felt when he opened it and said that it was the most beautiful tie he had ever seen.

"Too beautiful to wear," he announced enthusiastically as he kissed me on the cheek, closed the box, and put on his polka-dot tie.

What could I do? I served him a lot of soup in those days, hoping he might accidentally spill some on his polka-dot tie, but he never did. I tried spaghetti, but he must have known he was no match for spaghetti, and before he sat down to eat he removed his polka-dot tie. He really slopped up his shirt that night. I felt defeated as I looked over to see his tie hanging safely from another chair.

I don't know why I should have been surprised to find myself living with the banker I had married in the first place, and I don't suppose I should have minded. But I did. Perhaps it was some sort of moral deficiency on my part; perhaps *everything* was my fault. Maybe if I could have accepted him, really accepted Sergei for who he was, he would be someone else again. But for whatever reason, it didn't happen. Years came and went and I felt myself suffocating in a colorless marriage.

I arrived finally at that inevitable moment—that

moment of pure helplessness when all lies fail and the choice is clear. After all we had been through together I couldn't believe it was over. That night, with my heart in my throat, I informed Sergei that I was leaving. Darkness surrounded us as if there would be no tomorrow, but the next morning cruelly came and I awoke numb, not even daring to feel the consequences of my decision.

I stumbled to the kitchen to make coffee for my husband, perhaps for the last time. Immersed in my grief and all the small familiar tasks, I barely heard the strange footsteps behind me. Then, sensing that someone was there, I turned quickly to see. I gasped and my hands clasped my heaving chest as I saw Sergei the Attorney approaching me. He was wearing his new tie, and he announced judiciously that he would be enchanted to handle my divorce.

Time and Again

Seventeen years was a long time—too long, some said. Gerald had tried to forget, he'd had a few affairs, but they were brief respites, that was all. Work helped. It was hard to stay depressed delivering babies all the time, although sometimes it seemed a cruel fate to be helping create other people's families when his had been ripped from him so violently.

It was Thanksgiving. Like most nights since Mavis had died, Gerald had no place to go. As he walked home through the cold, empty streets, every sound echoed in the night. A man in a fedora passed him by—they ignored each other. He heard someone behind him and thought it was the same man but the footsteps seemed to be approaching rather than fading away. A slight hint of fear heated his neck and he turned. It was a girl, a white girl, a small wisp of a thing with blond hair hurrying toward him in the mist. Gerald continued to walk, waiting to hear her steps catch up and overtake him.

"Hey!" she called. "Wait up!"

He turned again, but kept walking.

"Wait! Wait! Yeah, *you*!" she said as he looked back at her once more with a perplexed expression.

He continued on, but slowly, allowing her to catch up.

"Hi!" she said excitedly, struggling to get her breath.

Gerald looked at her and smiled politely. What in hell is this about? he wondered. She was pretty in a mousy, Caucasian way and she carried a tote bag almost as big as she was. Still excited but now somewhat puzzled, she said, "Don't you recognize me?"

"Excuse me?"

"You don't. Oh my God." She looked hurt.

He wondered if perhaps she was one of the thousands of babies he'd delivered over the years. She looked to be around sixteen or seventeen years old but seemed somehow tired, burdened, something in the eyes.

"Why should I recognize you?" he asked.

"Damn, I was warned about this, but still I don't believe it."

"Look, miss, I don't know who you are," he said, quickening his step.

"Mavis," she said expectantly, pointing to herself with a proud smile.

Black as he was, Gerald blanched.

"That's not funny," he said. After all these years he still ached for her every night. Every night he imagined her lying next to him in bed; he could smell her. She was so real inside of him that he couldn't understand why she wasn't there. It didn't make sense. It pissed him off. The baby had lived for almost six months after Mavis, but then he had died, too.

"Is this some kind of joke?"

"I ain't laughin'," the girl said, now revealing a distinctly down-home Mississippi delta accent. Gerald felt all his muscles stiffen. Was he being blackmailed? That was his first thought. His second was that he had absolutely nothing to be ashamed of; his sense of guilt simply came from being Black in a white man's society. As successful as he was, he could never really shake the fear that one day there'd be a knock on his door and they'd take it all away.

"Look, girl, I don't know who you are or who

told you about—"

"Who you callin' 'girl,' boy?" she accused, huffing herself up and giving an impudent snap of her fingers. He pulled back and looked at her hard, deep in the face. Alabaster white. A few freckles on her nose, stringy blond hair and no hips. Mavis had some hips on her. No ma'am, this was not his Mavis.

"Look, little lady, I only meant . . . well, what right do you have?" He was confused, strange hopes stirred. "Did you know Mavis?" he asked suddenly.

"Know her? Honey, I must say I gave you more credit than this. I never knew you to be so fooled by superficialities, Gilly."

"Gilly. No one ever calls me Gilly."

"Not no more, maybe, but I did. So did your mama. Whatsa matter with you, man?"

He looked at her face. He had prayed so hard to have Mavis back. He didn't believe in miracles, but no one else knew his nickname.

"Turn around," he said, and she did, slowly, as he examined her slender form.

"Where's your ass, woman?" he said, allowing hope to overtake reason.

"I lost weight. They don't serve you no soul food, honey, you can bet *your* ass on that. And they done give me a white girl's ass to go with my white girl's body. What do you think?" She posed seductively.

He looked away, remembering himself. He was tempted to believe her, but reality was getting in the way.

"What do you want from me?" he asked, guarded once more and now getting a little angry. She looked hurt again. "How do you know so much about me, about Mavis?"

"Oh Lawd, they warned me that this might happen," she said, shaking her head, "but I said, 'No, no, not my Gilly. You'll see,' I told them. Well, aren't you makin' old Mavis look like a fool?"

"To whom?"

"What do you mean to who?"

"Whom," he corrected.

"To the other ghosts."

"Ghosts?"

"Shee-eet, baby, I died, right? Where you think I been, Club Med?"

"You're a . . . a ghost?"

"Honey, we all ghosts. But look at me now." She showed off her lithe body. "I'm as real as you are."

"Who are you?" he asked with a pained expression.

"I'm, I'm, uh—" She pulled her wallet out of her

bag and checked the driver's license. "Oh, that's right, I'm Crystal Baker. Still slips my mind every once in a while."

"Crystal Baker?"

"Cute, huh? Look, honey, I asked to be Black and they said, 'Are you crazy? Ain't you seen what's going on in the cities?' So here I am. Hitched here all the way from Darien, Connecticut."

Gerald sank down on the steps of the nearest building. He couldn't look at her anymore. He felt nauseated, and the setting sun reflecting off her pale white skin hurt his eyes. With his head in his hands he said, "I prayed for her to come back every night. Every night."

"I heard you, baby, I heard you," she said tenderly. "I wouldna come back if I hadna thought you wanted me."

Her voice.

"Say that again," he said, looking up.

"I say, I wouldna come back if I hadna thought—"

There could be no question about it—Mavis' chocolate-brown cotton-belt voice was coming right out of this milky white mouth.

He looked at Crystal but quickly looked away. The disparity of voice and corpus made him dizzy, as if he were caught in a clash between two worlds.

"Oh Lord," he said, holding his head.

"Whatsa matter, ain't you happy to see me, baby?"

"Oh Lord. Oh Lord."

"He heard you, too, baby. Who do you think arranged all this?"

"Oh Lord," he moaned.

"That's right, sugar. Now pull yourself together and let's go home."

"Home?"

"Honey, we sho 'nuff ain't goin' to my mama's for Thanksgiving supper, I can tell you that. I ain't seen my man for seventeen years, and before that I spent an eternity without a body. Now that I have one, I intend to make the most of it." She sat down next to him on the steps and put her slim white fingers on his thigh.

"Oh Lord."

"Now what is the matter with you, man?"

Except for "Oh Lord," Gerald was at a loss for words. Thoughts swam in his head, coming at him from all directions. Every once in a while he stole a quick glance at her—that was all he could take. It wasn't that he was afraid of ghosts—he didn't believe in ghosts—but there was no explaining this. Anyway, she'd said she wasn't a ghost anymore. But then who or what was she?

31

It was getting chilly. Gerald was shivering. Crystal put her arms around him and he warmed immediately. It had been such a long time since anyone had touched him, really touched him. No, no, he mustn't let such considerations affect his judgment.

"How old are you?" he asked.

"Seventeen."

"Oh Lord."

"And a half," she added quickly. "But, Gilly, I'm really, let's see, I'd be—two, three, four—I'd be forty-five this month."

Well, at least the problem had begun to take shape. He was fifty-one years old. Even if this were Mavis, even if he weren't hallucinating or losing his mind, he could not be expected to live with, to marry, a seventeen-year-old white girl.

"What would your mama say?" he asked.

"Which one?"

Her soul had been assigned to a nice, upper-middle-class family in Darien. "She won't be surprised I left— I think she suspects she's not my real mama anyway."

"So what *about* your real mama?" he insisted. "You think Mavis's mama would let me do this to the memory of her baby? If she found out I was with some little white child, she'd have me arrested for sure."

"After I came billions of light years to get back here, not to mention hitchhiking from Connecticut, how can you worry about what people think? Um um um, brother, you have some nerve. And after keepin' me up every night, howlin' like you was about to bust, and me tryin' to rest in peace? Do you think I wanted to come back here? Shee-eet, man, dead is dead! I was in no hurry to get back here."

"All right, calm down—the whole thing's a little weird, that's all. I mean, death . . . what *is* it? What is life, for that matter? Oh Lord."

"Grab hold of yourself, boy!"

"Ha! You come back here all dead and white and you tell *me* to grab hold of myself? You are really somethin'," Gerald said, shaking his head. But then he looked up, looked at her suspiciously. "That is, at least I *think* you're somethin'. Maybe you're nothin'. This is crazy, that much I know. Either *you're* crazy or *I'm* crazy. I mean, you are dead, woman. I buried you myself!"

"Guess again," she teased.

"Well, what is death then? What is it?"

"Not much, honey. But not half bad, either. Except for all them loved ones you leave behind howlin' and callin' your name. 'I'm dead,' I'd shout back, 'leave me be.' But you never heard me. 'How come I can hear you if you can't hear me?' I'd say, but you didn't hear that, either. If you ask me, you just wasn't listenin'. Never did listen to a word I said, anyhow."

"That's not true, baby." Gerald was thoughtful for a few moments. "But what's it like? If you have no body, how do you know you exist?"

"It's tricky."

"How?"

"How could I *not* know from all the racket y'all was puttin' up?"

"Is that all?"

She was quiet as she pushed a wisp of hair from her forehead and then drew her legs up under her skirt. "No. Well, I guess I'm hard-pressed to explain it." They both sat silently and then she added, "You just know."

"But how? You've got to tell me."

"I don't know. It's true you have no body. No one can see you; there's nothin' to see. I don't know, in a way that makes you feel *more* real, like you was burnin' with every ounce of energy you ever had."

"Burning? Like in hell?"

"Well, sort of, I guess. But like a star, too—one of heaven's golden stars."

"What about—" Gerald looked down at the pavement. "What about Eric?"

Her voice softened as she said gently, "He dead, honey, you know that."

"But so are you, so *were* you—whatever—I mean, where is he? Did you see him up there?"

"Up where?"

"Heaven."

"Who the hell said anything about heaven?"

"I thought you just said—"

"Never mind. It don't matter what-all you call it, it's all just a state of mind."

"And Eric?"

"He dead, honey."

"Forever?"

"Baby, I was a ghost, I wasn't God."

"Did you see him?"

"Who, God?"

"No, Eric."

"Nothin' to see."

"Did you . . . oh, I don't know."

"Yeah, yeah—once. I don't know how I knew it was him. But I felt him, I sure did, our little angel. And I said, 'Is that you, baby? Is that my baby?' You know, he couldn't talk yet anyway, but yes, I sensed him once."

"And he was okay?"

"Honey, he was dead. But all things considered, yeah, yeah, I think the boy will be just fine."

Gerald looked at her and suddenly felt his heart full as it hadn't been for seventeen years. He didn't know how, but this was his Mavis, that was for sure. He knew her heart. He wanted to hold her, but it was wrong to touch such a sweet young thing. He was afraid to touch her white skin.

"How come they didn't give you a new voice?" he asked.

"Now don't you get started on my accent," she chastised. "I know you always thought I talked too down-home ignorant for a big rich doctor like you."

"That's not what I meant. I was just wondering, that's all," he said, but he felt ashamed, for he knew she was right about the past. "Sugar, it's music to my ears," he said.

It was the first sign of tenderness he'd given her and it did not escape her attention. Looking into his eyes, she touched his cheek.

"You look tired, baby."

"Just old," he said.

"You ain't old. You just lonely. We'll fix that."

She kissed him on the mouth. He tasted her skinny

lips. He was used to some serious lips—these felt like a child's. He pulled back suddenly. Hell, she *was* a child. A white child at that. What in God's name did he think he was doing?

"Whatsa matter, baby? You don't like me anymore?" She looked at him sadly.

"I could get arrested," he said.

"Let's go home."

It was a bad idea; he knew it. "I guess we have no choice," he said, "unless . . ." His head was swimming, he felt nauseated. "Unless this is a dream. It'd make much more sense as a dream. And I've had some doozies since you left me."

"Yeah, I saw a few."

"You could see my dreams?" he said, slightly horrified.

"Well sure, the dream world—that's where we spirits live. We just have to tune in to whatever dream we want to be in. It's like TV—just change the channel. You'd be surprised how most people let you right in, too. Some dreams, you can even get in on the action. You, for instance. You always let me in, and we had a few good times together, didn't we, baby? Yes, indeed, a few fine nights."

"You mean you were really there?"

"I guess that all depends on what you mean by *really*. But yeah, I was there. Couldn't you tell?"

"Well, sometimes, right after you died, I did notice that my dreams seemed particularly real. So when I woke up I'd be confused when you weren't there. And angry, too."

"I heard you, honey. But I was flattered you didn't forget me."

"Forget you? I wish I could have. I mean, seventeen years is a long time."

"Don't try to tell me there were no other women. I know better."

"Seventeen years is a long time."

"And that fat bitch from the hospital you kept dreamin' about? You never did get your hands on that one, did you, lover?"

"Who? You mean . . . how'd you know I . . . don't tell me you could read my thoughts, too," he said, blushing.

"There are a few advantages to not havin' a body."

"That's cold, baby."

"Don't worry, I gave you plenty of privacy. You can't blame me for checkin' in every now and then to see what kind of no good you was up to. Fat Pearl, that's what I called her. Have your fun, I thought. I'll be back."

They were quiet for a moment as they watched the sun disappear.

"We can't set here all night, Gilly."

"Are you hungry?" he asked, trying to forestall the inevitable.

"Am I! I've been waitin' through seventeen years of chicken á la king for one plate of ham hocks and black-eyed peas!"

• • •

Kit's Soul Kitchen was still standing, and Kit nearly dropped a plate of ribs when he saw Gerald walk through the door.

"Well, lookee who's here," he said, grinning from ear to ear. "Come on out here, Luanne, and lookee who we got down here."

Pretty soon everyone in the little restaurant was staring at Gerald and Mavis. Except it was Crystal's transparent white skin they were staring at.

Even when they'd moved uptown, Gerald and Mavis still went back to the old 'hood to eat at Kit's every month or so. But Gerald never seemed to get there on his own after Mavis died.

"Well now, I won't ask you what you been doin' all these years," Kit said, winking and glancing suggestively at Crystal.

Gerald looked down. "She just wanted some ham hocks," he mumbled.

"Then you sure came to the right place. Come on in and set down. Make yourself to home, little lady, there you go. You're lookin' good, Gerald, real good."

"You too, Kit. The place looks the same."

"Can't complain," he said. "So what can I get you?"

Gerald was sweating by the time Kit finished taking their order.

"Here, honey, you ain't lookin' so good." Crystal held her napkin to his forehead, but he grabbed it from her and mopped his brow.

"Don't do that!" he said. "Don't touch me in front of everyone."

"No one's lookin'," she said gently, but then she glanced up at a dozen pair of black eyes.

Except for a few contented grunts from Crystal, they ate in silence. As Kit cleared their plates away, Crystal asked if he still made his famous sweet potato pie.

"I sure do."

"I'll have a piece of that delicious pie."

"Why'd you have to do that?" Gerald whispered after Kit had gone.

40

"Do what?"

"Ask him about his famous pie? You want him to know it's you?"

"I'm sure he thought you told me about it, that's all. But anyway, what's the big secret?"

"He'll think I'm nuts, that's what. 'The ol' guy finally done went off the deep end,' that's what he'll be telling everybody. Shit, maybe he's right. If you *are* a dream, why am I taking you for collard greens and sweet potato pie?"

"If I was a dream, would all these people be ogling me?"

"How should I know? Maybe you're *all* in my dream. Hell, they probably think *they're* dreaming, too—they're not used to seeing all that white skin in here."

"Sugar, you are too damn uptight. We are definitely going to have to do something about that attitude. Now, you hardly touched your ribs. Maybe you're hungry for somethin' else," she said, grinning.

"Stop talking like that," he said as Kit approached with the pie.

"This one's on me," Kit said, "but you two come back now, hear? Don't be such a stranger, Gerald."

• • •

"This ain't the Gerald I knew and loved," Crystal said, settling onto Gerald's couch. "Where's your soul? Where's your passion? Ain't you even glad to see me?"

He'd thought of almost nothing but Mavis all these years, waiting and waiting. Now that she was really here, or almost really here, he couldn't touch her. Her flesh, so young, firm, tender, so white—everything about it was forbidden. He felt his own skin like leather, the extra pounds around the belly. How could she want him, anyway?

"You're lookin' at me so strange," Crystal said.

"Well, you look pretty strange."

"You don't like me?"

"I like you fine, baby. It's just that you *are* a baby. Can't you see I'm an old man?"

"Close your eyes," she said. "What do I look like now?" She started to hum the song she always sang to him lying in bed at night; an old Negro spiritual her grandmother used to sing.

"Brown," he said. "Beautiful and brown with eyes dark as country soil and hair as black as night. And bosoms, real bosoms, and a nice big ass," he laughed.

"That's better. It's a matter of soul," she whispered and leaned over and kissed him sweet as eternity.

• • •

He and Mavis were in the country, down home in the Carolinas. Eric was with them. Gerald stood before his son with his arms stretched wide open as the boy struggled to his feet on fat wobbly legs and walked toward him. The sun shone on Mavis's smiling face as Eric picked up one foot after the other, placing it carefully on the ground, his face serious till he'd earned the joy of reaching his Daddy's arms. Scooping him up, Gerald whirled the child around, then, laughing, turned to Mavis. The smile died on his face. She was gone.

Gerald woke up. Frantic, he turned to Mavis fully expecting to find the customary emptiness beside him. But the sleeping body was still there. He reached over and felt the slender thigh of a young girl, and then he sat up, anxious and out of breath.

"Oh Lord," he said, "Oh Lord."

He saw Crystal's blond hair spilling off the pillow. He touched it, examined it with his fingers. It didn't even feel like hair.

Crystal rolled over sleepily and half opened her eyes.

"Mornin', sugar," she said.

He turned away.

"Whatsa matter?" she asked.

"I can't."

43

"Seems to me you already did. Yessir, honey, you sho 'nuff did."

"Oh Lord, I feel so ashamed."

"You did just fine, sugar. Nothin' to be ashamed of as far as I can see."

"What have I done? I'm an old man."

"You ain't lost a thing, baby."

"Stop talking like that. Why do you keep making it sound so dirty? You never talked that way before."

"Well, honey, like I said, it's been a long time."

"It's been a long time for me too, and you don't hear me talking dirty like that."

"It ain't dirty," she said. He could see her breasts over the sheets, small but shapely, with pink nipples.

"Who are you, anyway? Look at you," he shouted, throwing the blanket over her. "Cover yourself up."

He jumped out of bed.

"Who am I?" Crystal responded. "Who do you think I am? Don't I feel familiar? Didn't we dance together like we used to do?"

"I don't know. I guess so. I don't know."

"You need a little breakfast, that's all. I'll make you your favorite—walnut waffles. You still have that sorry old waffle iron we bought at the junk shop?"

"Yes. No. I mean, I have no time for waffles now.

And how did you know I liked walnut waffles? Who *are* you?" His eyes were wild.

"Let's not keep goin' over old ground. Seems to me you oughta just accept the inevitable and let's take it from there."

"Inevitable? Are you saying I have no choice? A man who has no choice is no better than an animal."

"Of course you have a choice," she crooned sweetly. "You can have whatever you want. I thought you wanted me."

He looked at her all curled up like a kitten in his bed. That bed had been empty for so long. He remembered her whispering in his ear last night as he came, and he was tempted to make love to her again.

"No!" he said emphatically. "I don't want you! That is, I do, but—no, no! I want Mavis. You're not Mavis. I hear her voice, but I don't see her. No matter what you say, no matter how you sound, no matter how we feel together, you're not Mavis. I sure enough don't know who you are," he said, his eyes flashing, "but you sure enough ain't Mavis!"

"It's a matter of soul," she said gently.

"You're trying to confuse me, I know you are. Talking so sweet in my ear I can't think straight. Who are you? Some kind of devil woman? Well, you know what? I don't care who you are anymore. I'm late for work."

"But I just got you back," she said. "I've been so lonely without you."

"You think I haven't been lonely? God, woman, how can I let you go?"

He ran back to the bed and caught her in his arms.

"You can feel in your soul that I love you," she whispered. "That's all that matters."

"Oh, baby," he sighed, the years of longing audible in his voice. He was melting. But it scared him and once again, as if he'd been burned, he jumped away, tossing her back against the pillow.

"You need me, baby," she purred. "You want me, sugar. I know you do."

"But *I* don't know! I don't know what I want!"

"Baby, you're just workin' yourself up into a state. Let's get you some breakfast. That oughta calm you down and help you think. Come on now, I tell you I know what you want—how about some of those waffles, sugar?"

"Save that syrup for your damn waffles!" he barked, surprising himself with the sudden harshness of his tone. Then just as suddenly he started to laugh; he'd finally gone off spinning in the confusion of his feelings. He had to laugh. The truth was, he no longer had any idea what he wanted. But he did know one thing: he didn't want waffles.

"What's so funny?" she asked worriedly.

"Waffles!" he roared, holding his belly.

"Waffles?"

He struggled to catch his breath. "I don't even *like* waffles anymore," he said, laughing through his tears. "Too much damn cholesterol, and too damn sweet!"

"I'll make eggs," she said.

"No, no, no. Here's how it is, baby."

Gerald grew suddenly sober and looked into Crystal's clear blue eyes. "Even if you are Mavis, you're not the Mavis I married, and it isn't because of your white skin or your blond hair or your skinny ass. It's because she's dead, it's because of these seventeen long years. It's because I'm not the same Gerald."

Crystal looked at him fearfully as he quietly sat down on the bed.

"I can't go back," he said gently. "It isn't you, it's time. Time won't allow it."

Mavis appeared to be paralyzed. She sat so still and grew so pale she might have been made of marble.

"Oh Lawd," she finally whispered. After a long pause she said, "What am I supposed to do now?"

"You have to go on and find a new life. You're young."

"But I've been waiting for you."

"I've been waiting, too. Looks like we've both been waiting for the wrong thing."

"Oh Lawd."

He looked at her with love. He could feel it now, but it was a different kind of love than he felt before. Sad. He patted her hand and held it warmly in his.

"I'm late," he finally said. She nodded.

Gerald went to take his shower. When he got back, Crystal was gone. Mavis was gone, too.

In My Own Words—
by God

••

I find it very odd that once man had created Me to be the embodiment of omniscience and wisdom, he never listened to what I had to say. "Oh God, Oh God!" all night long, and Me up here shouting answers into his deaf ears. I said it wasn't a good idea to kill, and he kills everything and everyone in sight. And that's just the beginning. I admit it gets to Me—eternity is hard to bear all alone, being alternately adored and ignored. A victim of monotheism, I am destined to live a solitary life. Sometimes I think of Zeus and his pantheistic revelries in the minds of pious Greeks and yearn for just a little of his fun.

All I really have to occupy My time is the Book. It is My own personal version of the Bible, a handbook specifically intended for God's use when learning how to deal with mortals. Its potential readership is admittedly small—indeed, nonexistent as long as I hold the job—but I have worked on it diligently since I was first conjured up, and it provides Me with some degree of solace.

The Book deals with the practical aspects of being God as well as the psychological problems of identity that are bound to plague someone who doesn't exactly exist in the first place. Take the issue of image. They think I look like a man, and sometimes I suppose I do, but mostly I think I'm what you might call a woman—or let's just say a "feminine vapor." I exist in the thoughts of others, changing forms as quickly as quarks and as fluidly as ocean waves. Somewhere along the line they latched onto this idea of My looking human, which of course is preposterous, a narcissistic flight of fancy on their part—and deep down inside they all know it. However, as I point out in Chapter 1—"A Guide to the Human Psyche"—this little illusion enables them to use their physical brains to envision a *meta*physical being—an admirable feat, to be sure.

The Book begins, "In the beginning, or shortly thereafter, man created heaven, fashioning it of poems and faith that played like music in his primal brain. It was beautiful and, all excited, he fell in love, with nothing in particular. How deeply fevered was his love, yet so big and hot and amorphous that he could not carry it in his heart. Hurling his fire skyward, he there worshiped it and feared it and called it God. Fire to fire, I could not help but rally to the call, and ever thereafter he has sought to recapture the fire he rejected. He knew it was his, he knew it was good, he just couldn't imagine what it was, for he tried to discover with his brain what only his heart could know."

Chapter 2. The Book goes on to advise God (should I have a successor) to be aware of man's ungovernable tendency to flatter Him, for He is only composed of lost parts of man's own identity. It can be the undoing of God, who should always remember that His very existence is questionable at best. In this "credulity clause," I warn the deity to be cautious of reverent praise, for if man has one bad day—a parking ticket or heavy rain—he will damn You remorselessly to hell, a place he created for just such occasions.

In Chapter 3, entitled "Call Me Yahweh," I write: "Man created God in his own image, but don't let this crimp Your style. Man has not yet created himself and is capable of things of which he has not yet dreamed. Why not dream them Yourself, and maybe he will, too? Be the God You were meant to be, go back to Your roots, back to when they called You Yahweh and held You more lovingly inside, tolerating Your fire with such respect that they wouldn't even dare pronounce You. You were elusive, ephemeral, You burned numinously in their brains with the riddle of existence. Your main job as ruler of the universe is to guide man back to this primary vision, a vision of translucent blindness vis-á-vis God.

"Do not be disheartened by his stubborn resistance to be shepherded in this way, or swayed by his efforts to create for You a slick persona. Two generations now have been praying to Charlton Heston, and if You try to whisper to them Your real and nameless name— 'Yahweh . . . Yahweh'—they get dizzy and nauseous and have to sit down. 'What the hell is this?' they exclaim and I reply, 'Don't worry, it's just the waters of oceanic time come to wash you clean in its mystery.' But they don't hear Me. They either reach for a drink or just wait for the sensation to pass and the image of Charlton Heston to realign itself in their minds."

I do get discouraged; once I became desperate and sent Jesus down to try to make My point. Not that I had any power over his actual incarnation—he was just a character in My Book who immediately transcended literary space/time and captured hook, line, and sinker the imagination of mankind. My only best seller, going strong now for two thousand years, he provides rare proof that man does sometimes hear what I say. Since I am just a facet of his imagination, he probably hears it all on some level, and on a good day we work together. Jesus was a good day; again, not implying that I created him, but as in any relationship it's hard to know just who's inventing whom.

Much of My time is now spent trying not to be seduced by the immortality thing, for I am flattered day and night. I try not to believe that I am the last and only God because I suppose there will be others to take My place. But in all modesty, I believe I have provided a worthwhile handbook for any who may be cast by accident into this divine light. The Book is unfinished, a work in progress, and I look ever forward to new revelations. I still dare to hope for answers to the knotty problems, like the origin of the fire that ignited man to create Me to begin with. Pondering this has often led to sleepless nights and My own helpless musing, looking past the sky and crying for mercy to some greater God, still undreamt of by man.

Lisa's Story

She heard their boots as they approached, clattering on the marble floor. The rhythm and pattern of their marching stood apart from the undifferentiated din of activity in the small suburban train station. It was not an unpleasant sound—like a troupe of tap dancers—but then she saw the guns.

Immediately, like a dream, things slowed down around her as if she were trying to stop time. The people went on buying their tickets and lugging their suitcases, getting their candy and cigarettes, their newspapers, but all in slow motion, never noticing what was about to happen—or had it already happened in the other realm of normally moving time? And then everyone scattered, running from the sound of bullets that had probably already killed them, dropping to the floor, squirming as they muttered their last pleas. Some were instantly still. And Lisa herself dropping to the ground by instinct, not because she'd been hit, although she couldn't be sure: the noise, the fear, and the dying were all bullets, too.

With her baby in her arms almost crushed between her pounding heart and the cold marble, she crawled, afraid to look around, sliding surreptitiously like a snake over the rocks of inert bodies till she made it to a little room off the main floor of the station. It was a small lounge with a torn, brown leather couch and heavy chairs to match, and two old vending machines with cardboard signs hastily scribbled: Out of Order.

She would be safe here. She stood up, her back hugging the wall, daring for the first time to look up. She hid the child's head with her cotton jacket. There was no one around, but she knew she wasn't free. There was no door besides the one she had entered, no other place to go. She waited there, hoping no one had seen her crawl in.

Clutching the baby tightly, Lisa put her lips against the soft down of his head. With a surge of fear she felt her blood prickling against the inside of her skin as she imagined herself back in the danger and commotion—a premonition maybe, for in the next instant two terrorists were upon her, pressing a gun into her gut. They were dark, Middle Eastern, a man and a young woman with long nails painted red. Lisa had never seen a machine gun before and its dark menace stunned her.

She froze, defenseless, and Gus, sleeping cuddled inside her jacket, seemed like a dandelion on a battlefield. She couldn't bear for their eyes even to rest upon him, as if that in itself would be lethal to him. She stood paralyzed against the wall with her eyes wide open, afraid to move.

The man and woman stopped and watched her, one on each side, examining her strange behavior. They were obviously amused as they circled around their prisoner, poking her and whispering to each other about her.

Lisa was an ordinary woman with a plain face, a nose slightly bulbous at the tip, and thick lips. Her lips would have been described as sensuous on some other face, but on hers they were just thick. Her hair was thin and fine, light brown, almost blond, the color of camomile tea; straight, clean, and shiny, it was neatly pulled back into two functional-looking barrettes at the sides of her head. Her hazel-green eyes, normally hungry and alert, were now dazed.

Thoughts raced through her brain—why hadn't she left her mother's house sooner and caught an early train home? She hadn't even wanted that extra cup of coffee. What kind of mother was she, what kind of instincts, she chastised herself, as if she should have sensed the danger ahead.

They were mocking her as they commented back and forth in some kind of Arabic tongue. Her life was in the balance, yet these people were enjoying themselves with a kind of frothy good humor and easy laughter one would not expect of terrorists. The woman came up close to Lisa and blew in her face. She automatically blinked and her captors laughed. The man walked over to Lisa and teasingly put his lips on hers. With no other means of escape, Lisa sank to the floor, collapsing like a rag doll on top of Gus, cradling his head as they went down. Everything else she was carrying dropped from her arms; her purse, a small notebook, some loose pages that scattered, fluttered down, and settled around her like a first snow. It was her story.

For years Lisa had felt a vague sensation, in the beginning only an intimation, like an itch whose source can't be located. It made her do strange things—ride trains all night long or sleep with men who abused her, men who tried to possess her spirit. She pretended she loved them and would live with one of them for a while, then finally betray him, as if to be loyal to the truth. She was caught once and beaten for her indiscretion, but she could not defend herself since she thought she deserved it.

It all seemed so futile, and Lisa swore off love entirely for a while before she met Lee. When Gus was born Lisa felt happy, as if the world had just been born and they were the only ones in it—she and Gus and Lee—but it was up to her to provide a life for Gus, a reality, and she had to admit that she didn't know what that was, for the past haunted her in the dark eyes of her old lover as he came after her with jealous rage. How could she get free of her own memory? It stalked her like a nameless, faceless, insatiable beast. She wanted to cry out, but to whom? And what would she say? She was like a prisoner helplessly immured within her own walls, plagued constantly by her desire to be free. What kept her from going mad she did not know; what was driving her mad was equally unknown, and the dark comfort of suicidal thoughts were balanced only by her responsibility to her son. There was no relief. Confused and dizzy from indecision, she had finally sat down, considering nothing but her next breath, and written this story.

So maybe it wasn't a masterpiece; she was free. Now it lay on the floor, strewn about like a dismembered body. And there she lay, torn apart by fear, ready at any second to feel the sting of a bullet. How long could she stand it? Fearing that it could only end one way, she held onto Gus and fought her wish for it to be over.

The woman approached Lisa and kicked her callously in the leg, then circled around to the other side. Lisa steeled herself for another kick but instead the woman leaned down and rifled through the pages of her story. What could they possibly want with her? Was she a hostage? What would they do to her? Her imagination was racing as the woman picked up one of the pages.

"What's this?" the woman asked. Then she began to read aloud: "'William walked out on the terrace and sighed deeply. His breath was a white frozen cloud in the black night. His wife, Grace, followed a few moments later, clearly upset, and asked William what was wrong.'"

She read the words stiffly and with a thick accent, although she obviously spoke English. The air of terror mixed strangely with the world of fiction, like mismatched strangers on a blind date. The woman laughed. Is she laughing at my story? Lisa wondered defensively. She winced to hear her words in the mouth of her potential executioner.

"Stop reading that, Sanam," her comrade said in a gruff voice, but she continued on with a smile:

"'You aren't pining over that woman, are you?' Grace asked, her eyes hard. William was silent, his brows furrowed as he looked out from the veranda.'"

But the woman he had called Sanam had pronounced it "pinning" and "voronda." She was butchering the language with her illiterate pronunciations. Lisa bit her lip. It was killing her to hear it.

"'William's square jaw was set. His eyes barely blinked. So proud, so stubborn; when he got that look Grace knew there was no way to get through to him. Something really must have happened between him and that woman, Grace thought. She put her hand on his shoulder, but he didn't respond. She turned and walked inside. Picking up her raincoat, she glanced back at her husband's slender, elegant silhouette against the cityscape, and left.'"

Sanam stopped reading. Lisa knew she had come to the end of the page and she heard Sanam rustling around on the floor trying to find the next one.

"Sanam, come over here. Quick!" the man ordered. Then, lapsing back into their own language, they bickered back and forth. Finally he told Sanam to guard Lisa while he went outside. What were they waiting for? Reluctantly Sanam dropped the pages she had gathered and took up her watch. As he left she called out, "Abul, give me the gun!" They exchanged a few more words in Arabic and finally she laughed, saying, "I need a gun more here than you do to go to the bathroom," and he came back and handed her the machine gun. He said he'd be back in a minute and left.

Lisa's fear slackened enough to be aware of physical discomfort, her leaden arms and legs. Gus was so quiet that Lisa was afraid he was dead, but then she felt the soft heartbeat and the faint breath from his tiny nostrils against the hollow of her throat. Miraculously he was still asleep, and although Lisa feared she might crush or suffocate him, she didn't dare move.

Abul returned, saying a few words to Sanam that Lisa couldn't understand. Were they talking about her, about what they were doing there? They laughed together, flirtatiously, Lisa thought, and continued to go in and out of speaking English. Sanam said they should have stopped to get bread, a sandwich, at least a cup of coffee—she was starving. But he said to shut up and stop complaining, and he grabbed the gun from her hands. Sanam started to hum. Once more Abul told her to be quiet. They were silent for a while and then Sanam said, "Imagine, Abul, back home the summer festival has just begun. Do you think Jelal and Zena are there now?" He grunted. "What do you think they are doing?" she continued. "Dancing? Drinking? I can just see them, can't you? Last year—"

"Can't you be quiet?"

"What can I do? I miss home."

"We can never go back. If not the police, your husband will kill me."

"He will understand in time. Eventually he would—"

"You talk too much!"

"I know. My mother used to tell me the same thing. I can't help it. Why do you think that is?"

"How should I know? Why don't you shut up and think about it?"

She started to say something else but he told her to shut up and she did. Abul went to sit in one of the old leather chairs at the corner of the room, his gun trained in a straight line upon Lisa and the door.

Sanam wandered back over toward Lisa and

picked up a few of the scattered pages of the story. "Eight, seven, three," she read aloud as she picked them up. She had just read page four. She stopped, trying to decide whether she should go back and read page three or go on and look for five. She picked up page five with the next handful and read: "'There was a knock at the door.'"

"Shut up, Sanam!" Abul barked.

"What's it to you?" she barked back, and she continued to read the story: "'William went to the door thinking Grace had returned, but when he opened it, there stood Denise. She was radiant in her white fur, and William did what he could to control his feelings.'"

"Oh God," Abul moaned. She read on.

"'It was no use. Whatever hostility existed between them in that awkward moment disappeared as Denise walked in and fitted herself against William's body.'"

Sanam let out a little sigh of longing.

"'But as quickly as William had melted, he turned to ice again,'" Sanam read dramatically, "'and stretched her away from him with his long, slender arms.'"

It was the end of the page. Sanam went hunting on her hands and knees for page six.

Jumpy and distracted, Abul said, "Sanam, do you

think they'll show up like they said? They should be here already."

"Of course they'll show up. They want the money, don't they?"

"How long do we wait?"

"As long as it takes."

I'm a hostage, Lisa thought.

"What about the police?" Abul said, nervous, almost whining.

"Abul, you have no faith. You have no patience. Ah! Here it is," she said, and bent down to pick up page six.

As Sanam started to read, Lisa thought, "This is ridiculous," for she had almost begun to enjoy hearing her story read aloud. She had adjusted her ear to accommodate Sanam's accent, and the sound of her own words had something of a calming effect on her, which under the circumstances was as remarkable as it was welcomed. Forgetting her fear for a moment, she moved her arm to cushion Gus's head, and before she knew it Abul's gun was jabbing her in the ribs.

"Where the hell do you think you're going, lady?" he snarled. The muzzle of the gun felt cold through her cotton blouse and hard against her ribs. Tears rolled from her eyes and fell against the side of Gus's head.

She wanted to cry out, to protest, but she was mute.

"That's better," Abul said with an extra jab. Walking back to his corner, he sat, balancing himself on the back of the chair, his feet on the seat, the machine gun resting on his knees.

"'Denise was shocked at such treatment from the man she loved and who supposedly loved her. She did not know what had come over him. What had she done to deserve such rejection?' That's what I'd like to know," Sanam commented, fascinated.

"She probably talked too much," Abul said wryly.

"Very funny, darling. 'Denise fought back her tears but they flowed in heavy rivulets down her expressionless face. William had turned into some kind of robot, a creature without a heart, and his eyes were as cold and dark as iron.' That prick," Sanam said.

"What are you talking about?" Abul retorted. "The bitch probably screwed him over somehow."

"How would you know? You haven't even been listening."

"How would *you* know?" he countered. "You never read the beginning of the story."

"Well, just wait and see, that's all. I know a louse when I see one. So let's see, where was I?"

To Lisa's dismay, Gus began to squirm. He'd surely

wake up soon and then it would be all over. They'd shoot him, shoot them both. Lisa could hardly stand it anymore. Both her arms were asleep; little by little her body was turning into a piece of dead matter and she wouldn't be able to get up if she had to. She wouldn't be able to hold her baby.

"'Denise dried her tears and looked hard at William's face. Then she started to laugh, surprising even herself. William looked positively shocked, and then offended. She could be a bitch when she wanted to, he thought.'"

"See, I told you," Abul said.

"*He* thought. It said, *he* thought, *he* thought, that's what *he* thought. We still don't know what really happened."

"Well, go ahead then," Abul said, impatient.

"'He could be such a prick, she thought. . . .'"

"It doesn't say that," Abul sneered suspiciously.

"It certainly does say that. See? Right here," and she brought it over to him, pointing and reading with careful emphasis, "'He could be such a prick, she thought.' See? Anyway, 'Insulted, Denise wheeled around to depart, her white ermine swooshing about her as she turned.'"

"What's that?" Abul said with alarm.

"It's a little animal they make coats out of."

"Not that, you fool! I heard something—maybe the cops—or Ezrahi's guys. Put that damn thing down," he said, gesturing to the story with the tip of his gun.

"You're hearing things, Abul."

"Get that cunt off the floor—come on, get her over here."

"Come on, sweetie," Sanam said in a tough voice. "Rise and shine."

She nudged Lisa with her foot, then kicked her, but Lisa wouldn't budge. They'd take the baby, they'd kill her, she mustn't move. She couldn't move. Who was Ezrahi?

"I think she's asleep. Maybe she's dead," Sanam said, throwing her head back with a deep, throaty laugh. "Died of fright," she said. Then more softly she added, "Ah, let her be."

"Shh! Listen," Abul said.

"I don't hear anything," Sanam said after a silent minute.

"Let's go out to the south exit where the others are stationed," Abul suggested. "We should have covered the north exit."

"No one ever uses it—it's locked from the inside. They're all there where they should be. If they'd been caught, we would be, too. Where's page seven?" Sanam asked as she rustled through the papers.

"But they could have left, left us here," Abul said.

"Why would they do that? Faith, Abul, faith. Ah, here it is."

"Alright, alright," and after a pause, Abul commanded, "Read!"

"'What was William hiding? Denise wondered. He must be hiding something or he wouldn't be acting this way. She started to put her hand out to him to try to reach across the glaciers in which he had drifted away. But almost before she could move he had pulled a gun on her.'"

Abul laughed nervously. Sanam's eyes widened, her face became flushed.

"'Denise looked stricken. The muscles of her face went limp, her color drained away. She felt she had already been shot. But you love me, her eyes seemed to cry out. How could it be? Who had she been loving all these years? she wondered. The past was curling up and being eaten away like the pages of a burning book. Nothing was what it had pretended to be, the past was dying as she herself faced death at the hands of her own lover.' Wow," Sanam said quietly, and Abul shook his head with disgust. But he gestured for her to continue.

"'William gestured toward Denise with his gun, motioning her toward the bedroom. Her tomb, the site of so much pleasure. The poetry in life astounded her. When they reached the bed she became afraid that he would rape her. The horrible thought sobered her and gave her the presence of mind finally to ask him why. Why was he doing this? With fire in his eyes he explained that he loved her too much to let her be with anyone else. But I love you, she protested, confused. It was he who was married. She had no wish to be with anyone else. How could he be sure, he wanted to know. He must have certainty. She told him just to look into her eyes and have faith. But of course he couldn't. His eyes were cold and blind—hardened by jealousy and fear. He had lost his mind, and she had lost her man, worse, her dreams—perhaps worse still, her illusions. What was there to live for? She asked him softly for one more kiss, to die with. He laughed nervously but came slowly forward to embrace her. Without even thinking, Denise lunged at him and tried to grab the gun. William was caught off guard, and when she dived down and bit his hand, he released the gun.'"

"What a fool!" Abul moaned, shocked. Sanam read on.

"'Shaking, Denise pointed the gun at him. He looked at her, soft and lovely in her jewels and ermine, looked at her arrogantly, daring her to pull the trigger, knowing she couldn't do it.'"

"She won't," Abul said with disdain.

That was the end of page nine. "Where's page ten?" Sanam asked eagerly. Lisa froze inside. She had gotten stuck there after Denise wrested the gun from William; she didn't know if she should have her kill him or what. There was no page ten. It had not been written.

Sanam searched in vain. There were hardly any pages left on the floor by now and when she had gone through them all she said again, "Where's page ten?" But this time she addressed her question to Lisa. Lisa was afraid to tell Sanam the truth about page ten, and her silence inflamed Sanam's rage. Abul came over and ordered Lisa to answer. When she was still silent, he stuck the gun in her back and said, "Get up!" She had no choice but to do as he said, so with Gus in her arms, her body rendered clumsy by fear and an hour of immobility, Lisa struggled to her feet.

"Okay, lady, where's page ten?" Abul sneered.

"I don't know," she stammered, afraid to hear her own voice—as if, once exposed, that too would be a target for their violence.

"Who wrote this story?" Sanam asked.

"I did."

"You did?" Sanam was impressed. "So where's page ten?"

"There is no page ten."

"It's not over, is it?" Sanam asked worriedly.

"No. Not over. Well, I don't think so."

"Well, then?"

"I'd have to write it," Lisa said.

"So write it," Abul snapped.

"But I don't know what happens. I haven't written it yet."

"Never mind writing," he ordered, "Just tell it to us."

Getting frustrated at their lack of understanding, Lisa said, "I can't."

"Oh, you can't, eh? How about if I give you a little incentive?" Abul said, holding the gun to Gus's head. Sanam looked uncomfortable and said softly, "Abul." He paid no attention.

The baby began to squirm. Lisa felt insanity storming in her mind at the thought of Gus's blood in her hands. She felt her body scream, but stood calmly before Abul. She noticed Sanam looking at Gus with maternal eyes; then she asked Lisa, woman to woman, if she thought Denise would really kill William. Lisa admitted that she didn't really know if Denise had it in her. That's what had held up the story in the first place. Abul demanded once more to know. "You're the writer," he said, "Tell me or I'll shoot."

Sanam wanted to know the outcome of the story. With Abul it was something else. He was crazed, edgy; the situation had obviously gotten to him. He'd been waiting, waiting too long, and his faith had run out. He had to do something, take action, and Lisa could tell that he was enjoying her fear and his own cruelty. The threat, the smell of blood, had drowned his fear.

"I'll ask you one more time, lady," he snarled.

"Abul, there is no reason—" Sanam began, but Abul snapped, "Shut up! Since when do you tell me how to run things?"

As Lisa saw the cold look in his eye, she knew that he could really kill her, and her fear escaped the tenuous control in which she'd kept it harnessed. As if sensing this in his mother, Gus awakened with a shriek. Abul was shocked by the sound and would have started shooting had not Sanam intervened in that brief moment between shock and reflexive violence. Moving instinctively, she wrested the gun from Abul's hands and turned it upon him. The baby's wailing underscored the accumulated terror of the group. Abul looked as if he had just been awakened from a sound sleep in an unfamiliar room. Lisa was too frightened to feel relief and rocked Gus in her arms, hoping to calm him, as Sanam stood holding a gun on Abul. He looked at her, her pretty face, her painted nails, looked at her arrogantly, as if daring her to shoot.

"You wouldn't," he said.

Sanam looked at him, confused. She looked at the baby and at Lisa. Their eyes met in fear and then she motioned Lisa toward the door.

"Go," she said.

Gus had stopped crying. Lisa quickly gathered up the pages of her story and stuffed them under her arm. She nodded gratefully at Sanam. There were no words to say what she felt, and with a last fearful glance at Abul's puzzled face she hurried out the door.

Lisa headed for the unguarded north exit. So far it looked clear. She was trembling, her heart pounding as she forced the door open and felt the summer heat rush toward her and surround her. She wasn't safe yet, but she was out, she was free, and her lips curled into a slight smile.

She began to run, holding Gus's arm so tightly

that her fingers hurt, and when she released them there were red handprints on his soft skin. She ran for blocks, looking back at the train station every few seconds until she was sure there was no one following. She kept running all the way to town, all the way home where she knew Lee would be waiting.

Before she opened the door of the apartment, Lisa stopped to catch her breath. Gus's ingenuous eyes were fixed on hers as she smoothed his hair. The story was tucked securely under her arm, lodged between her baby and her body, and as she guided the key into the lock, she smiled. They had liked her story.

The Poet and the King

The king called for Daneus, the court poet, to fill his ears with new thoughts. The poet came before the king and all his courtiers but informed them regretfully that he had no thoughts today. Today he had no words, his head was filled with clouds and the vague sounds of a crowd of angry people, and children crying, hungry and begging for food. All these trespassers through the serenity of his mind kept stepping on the flowering of fresh words.

The king was irate. He depended on his poet to forge a clearing in his own cluttered brain. Once more he tried to coax from the poet a word or two of beauty to transport him to a sky painted by the feathers of birds. Daneus explained that his muse was on vacation, but the king would hear none of it and the poor poet sat quietly with his head in his hands. He sat for an hour as the king, burning with anticipation, watched him.

"Well? Well?" the king finally demanded, for he had not the patience of the poet, who was willing to wait forever, if necessary, for the return of his muse.

"Uh, let's see. . . ." said Daneus.

"Yes? Yes?" his majesty said expectantly.

"I—I—no, I can't."

"But you must! I order you!"

"It's not possible."

"I demand a poem!" his sovereignty bellowed.

"You don't know this woman," Daneus explained. "She is very headstrong, she answers to no one, not even kings."

"Ha! We'll see about that! But *you*! She has you neutered and crawling after her like a dog. You are a spineless slave to a woman, and one who does not even exist at that! This is a disgrace. I will not have as my court poet such a pitiful man. Off with his head!"

The king's guards swooped down on either side of Daneus like the wings of a great vulture to carry him away.

"Wait! Wait!" he screamed in desperation. "I will give you a poem!"

"Ah, that's better," the king sighed, for he did so love the mellifluous voice of Daneus. He sat down happily to listen, with a dreamy look in his eyes, transported by the thought of being transported.

Daneus was trapped. He did not want to betray his muse by uttering false words, nor did he want to die and so, boldly, he stepped forward. Grasping the lapel of his cloak with his left hand, he assumed his usual position of recitation.

"The, uh, no, wait. Let's see. Okay, the wind—"

He stammered, he stopped, he struggled to find even one word. One word, that was all he needed, but he could not find it—not the right word, an honest word, a word that could turn his own heart into a bird on the wings of which he, the king, and all his court could fly. Where was his muse? Only she could get him out of this mess. Only she knew the way. His muse had connections with God, whose words she translated and passed on to him. It was easy, really; all he had to do was listen. Of course, listening to the muse was not at all like listening to normal voices, which were audible and therefore much easier to hear. The muse spoke silently and only to those who believed she was speaking—that was all it took to hear her. There were dangers involved, however, considerable dangers. For if one truly believed, one ran the risk of becoming deaf to all that was formerly audible. The world itself could easily disappear under these circumstances, for the next thing one knew one's eyesight had failed along with his senses of taste, touch, and smell. It had happened to some of the best poets of the court. Carnaevon the Great, who had lived in the kingdom of Cyrus XVI, had completely ceased to exist, except in his own mind and that of his muse. Disembodied as such poets were, no one would have known of their existence at all had it not been for the beautiful poems they left every morning on the king's pillow.

Daneus thought of Carnaevon the Great, whose legend was so well known throughout the modern world, and he felt ashamed, the false words still burning in his throat. The king sat up, dismayed at the silence, and demanded to know the cause of the delay.

"I—I—" the poet stammered.

"What is it? What's wrong? Do you have a poem or not?"

Daneus hesitated, and the king, discouraged, motioned mercilessly to his guards once more. Once more they closed in on the dejected poet, who threw off their grip and blurted out,

"I am waves on an ocean shore. . . ."

"Yes, yes? Go on," the king urged, his eyes brightening.

"And birds flying to distant shores."

"Ah," the king sighed, preparing for deliverance.

> "I am the tracks of sandpipers
> writing in the sand
> ephemeral messages
> of eternity
> and death."

"Bravo! Bravo!" the king shouted, and his courtiers echoed his approval. Even the pages and the guards ferociously applauded the conscience-stricken poet. He had proceeded on his own, without his muse, to write a respectable poem, a poem applauded by a king. Proudly he bowed. He had accomplished no small feat today; after all, he had saved his hide. He bowed, and bowed again lower, and again lower and lower, and a last time lower to the appreciative crowd, until he fell to the ground and died.

Literary Lovers

Poetry sprang from her loins like a hungry lioness. Women like Bertha were raw material for the love of poets. She was their paper, she was the pen through which they poured their ink.

In one of the Pisan cantos, Ezra Pound referred to her as a "kallipygous Sienese female," though she'd never been to Siena. The passage sent her directly to her dictionary, where she was forced to spend most of her days. But women like Bertha gravitated toward genius, she swam in its seas; the rest were barnacles on her soul. She'd never forget her days at Muzot. Rilke was always inspiring, like that first transcendent night of love. "What small child, rolled in his own blanket of childhood, could feel the fire his mother walked on, burning her feet, her screams following him all his life?" he'd asked her the next morning before she had her coffee. "Good question," she'd said, neither understanding him nor believing he understood himself, but totally convinced of his sincerity. Eventually, she realized she'd been dumped by one of the greatest literary figures of all time, but he'd let her down gently on a pillow of poems, where she slept until she could stand to awaken.

She got one more letter before he died:

You have left some creature behind whose face is mine but who sings with your soul, dancing still around the fountain where we are both

Eternally Wet,
Rainer

What kept her from running back as fast as she could get a plane to Switzerland? Money.

Then he died, ever flesh in her memory, for he had sent her a copy of the sonnets and elegies, the last outpouring of his genius, which she knew had turned on him and killed him. Alone, Bertha drowned her sorrow reading Socrates and eating popcorn. Twisting her heavy heart around the great Greek's heavy brain, she felt light, aroused again by the threat of perfection. In Plato's mouth she found moist words to irrigate her mind. Poems of her own arose, dragging her toward heaven to meet him.

Heaven was a disappointment—there was no one there. Loneliness was magnified by the presence of beauty and exaltation. Everything shone in this light, even darkness and ugliness and grief. She walked the formal gardens of literary lore, she walked on marble, the objective, slippery edges of great shiny minds. Could poetry possibly survive in the suburban clime and rough flagstone paths of prosaic modern life? In her lap the *Duino Elegies* stared at her as if from another world. Had Rilke ever really loved her? She, the poet's delight, full of sex and centuries of meteoric, metaphoric love; she with the buoyancy of myth and the tits of a movie star. Muse of muses, she was out of work. She was out of her mind. Eliot came and went and not since then had she been filled with the explosions necessary for transcendence (and truthfully he was a bit too depressed for her taste, no offense to his literary bequest).

Huntress, she kept moving toward the light on Diana's sturdy legs, but the times refused to cough up another genius for her to mold. Oh, the loneliness of the single muse used to dual journeys in burning brains. Combing future universes, she finally found a gifted little boy who agreed to venerate her after he looked up the word *venerate* and made her promise he could also fuck her. "In due time," she said, "if you work hard and think of nothing but me, and never let me stop dancing where your heart holds itself empty."

"Okay," he said, without a clue as to what she was talking about, but he'd promised, and agreements are binding though one knows not to what he is bound.

She nursed him on ambrosia when most boys were drinking rotgut. She rubbed his nose in ugly reality to show him what Keats meant when he said, "Beauty is truth, truth beauty"—that was all he needed to know—but she taught him to take a pie in the face, just in case, and he grew up to be a cross between Christ, Rilke, and Nijinsky, but with a better sense of humor. He grew ever younger with the years. Dreams and dreams began to come and fetal dreams never stopped coming, though he never dreamed that Bertha was his pillow. She was hidden in his yearning, and in his ideals. She was flawed perfectibility and the eternal road. In time his own flaws came and hit him behind the knees and he fell at Bertha's feet. Finally he could see all that she had given him, but still preferred to claim the glory for himself—people are like that—

and Bertha had no choice but to leave, abandoning the hopes she had aroused in a future hungry for new poems. She kept hoping anyway. Perhaps if the boy were lucky, wisdom would someday take another crack at him and finding him a suitable host, plague him with the love of Bertha, and with poems immemorial.

Leda July's Flight

Home was so safe I thought I was dead. Mom always had supper on the table at six o'clock sharp and it always included canned vegetables and an unidentified red punch. The sickly sweet smell of it comes back to me whenever I'm in the presence of meat loaf. What was it, cherry? Raspberry? Or the juice of some justly forbidden fruit?

My given name is Leda July—a bit much, I think, for the offspring of Bill and Edna Ruskin of Tooele, Utah—but with me being their only child I guess when they named me they wanted to make it count. Daddy called me Swan because of the myth about the god who takes the form of a swan and fucks this lady named Leda.

The rest of life was more prosaic. Other than the daily dependable smells of childhood it was as if I had

no childhood at all, and when I moved out at age sixteen I felt I was leaving nothing behind. No memories,
no regrets, just a lifetime of well-regulated habits
coated with the Nutrasweet of good intentions.

I was an artist. Not a whole lot else really mat-
tered. I didn't even mind feeling nothing—maybe I
knew what was in store if I had felt the full impact of
life. For now, all I had was freedom, and that's a big
feeling at sixteen, as big as the world that was opening before me.

I carried only the tan and white checkered valise that
used to belong to Uncle Irwin. In it were some clothing,
lots of pencils and drawing paper and lots of socks. I
didn't want to spend my freedom washing socks.

I had my savings—$147.64—from my job helping
Daddy at the hardware store. It bought me a bus
ticket to Santa Fe, a hot pretzel, and a night at the Y
with plenty to spare. I wasn't even scared. I wasn't.
The next day I got a job as a waitress in a greasy
spoon. I told them I was eighteen and they bought it
without flinching.

"You slung hash before, kid?" Rosie asked. I was
honest. I said no, and that was fine with her. They
paid me nothing anyway, and I was a damn good
worker. At sixteen you can put your whole heart and

soul into slinging hash or anything that'll make you seem older, because you're only pretending to be older. When you get to be Rosie's age, though—say forty or fifty—you really *are* slinging hash and you know it and you can recognize that it's not so exciting. Reality can put quite a damper on things, but I was in no danger of that.

Letters from home were always the same, begging me to return. My folks knew where I was but they wouldn't just come get me, it wasn't their way. They would never take such a firm stand on an issue. My determination, even when I was a kid, struck them as something so alien that they were in awe of it and frightened to challenge it. It was either God or the devil incarnate in my being and they weren't about to truck directly with either one.

Mom wrote me about the delicious apple crumb pie she'd baked—a kind of lure, I figured, and I wrote her about all the delicious pies Rosie baked—a kind of tart retaliation I guess you could say. Daddy didn't have much to write but he added that my room was "ready and waiting for my Swan anytime she cares to return."

I knew I was too young to leave but I had no choice. I'd read the books. Artists were supposed to lead exciting lives—Van Gogh, Picasso, Gaugin. I didn't have the fare to Tahiti, but I was determined to be a real artist.

Sante Fe was very clean, except for Rosie's Grill. There wasn't any dirt outside, the streets you could eat off of, and the air was so clean you felt you could touch the pastel mountains surrounding us. Everything was as clear as my head wasn't. Most of the time my head was like the inside of the Grill—thick, steamy, and spattered with hot fat.

Things were happening in Santa Fe. On my days off I hung around the museum or the galleries; we had nothing like that in Tooele. But mostly I painted or drew. I could only afford watercolors and did intense, precise landscapes of the Sangre de Christos or moody, watery portraits of Rosie and Al. I signed them and Rosie hung them on the walls above the tables with prices under them. The regular customers remarked how I had captured Rosie and Al to a "T," a perfect likeness, they said. And Gunther Graves, who'd secretly been in love with Rosie for years, offered to buy one of her for five bucks even though it already had grease stains on the neck. They let me keep the money, though I'd given them the picture as a gift. I'm never one to let an opportunity slip by, so I offered to paint a portrait of Mr. Graves, too. "Sure," he says and we planned to meet for a sitting the next day at his paint store.

Well, I got there and he lets me in but the store is all closed up. Gunther wants to pose nude and that's where the trouble starts. I didn't know what to say— I'd never had cause to learn how to say no, so I said okay, but I regretted it the minute I saw his pubic hairs peeking through the slot in his boxers. I'd never seen anything so black in my life, like a big grizzly bear hiding in a deep dark woods, ready to pounce. In a second it emerged naked from the woods and Gunther pounced and I ran away, grabbing my watercolors but leaving my brushes lying all over the floor.

I still thought this portrait thing was a good business proposition. I just had to be more selective about my customers. I asked Rosie if I could peddle portraits outside the Grill. "Why not?" she says. "It'll attract business." So on my day off there I am in front of Rosie's waiting for a catch. It seems the art lovers were somewhere else that day and I sat outside till closing just doing landscapes and cityscapes. I crossed the street and did a picture of Rosie's Grill and the next day gave it to Rosie to hang on the wall. She was impressed. "Thanks, dearie," she said. She liked me and so did Al, though it was subtle with him. "You want a chocolate malt, kid?" he'd say around four o'clock. He always made them extra thick.

Mom still wrote asking me to come home. Daddy still called me Swan. I almost couldn't remember what they looked like except that every once in a while their faces would sort of spark behind my eyes like a flash-bulb—stiff, hard poses for some ancient snapshot.

I was not oblivious to the romantic image of the suffering, starving artist and though I was well-fed and *too* oblivious to be suffering much, I played the part well. I read Jung, *Siddhartha,* and *The Bhagavad-Gita* and spent long hours alone communing with nature and contemplating man's purpose. After a few months I noticed that no one else could see the total groovy romance of my existence and around the same time I noticed I was lonely. What I needed was a friend. Everyone needs a friend, even if it's just to witness your misery.

Della and I became really close. She worked next door at the laundromat, making change for the machines, wiping up water, and collecting lint and stray socks. She'd come in to Rosie's for coffee and doughnuts on her breaks, or for lunch if she forgot to pack one. We'd chatter away in between her teasing

Al in a flirty way. She was older than me, nineteen, and I looked up to her for it. She was beside herself with admiration for me, a real artist. I did lots of sketches of her, her heavy eyebrows, her slightly crooked nose, her thick blond hair that was pulled back into a low ponytail from which stray hairs escaped around her face. The main thing you could say about Della was she loved to laugh, and when she did her eyes flashed with something dark and mysterious. Della was not exactly plump, but "healthy," and her pink uniform gapped in the front over large breasts, more like a chest than two distinct breasts. Did I say she liked to laugh?

Della was married already. Her husband, Weston, was twenty-four years old—a real man. He owned Wes's Gas Station. I told Della I was only sixteen. She was shocked, which I loved, and she promised not to tell Rosie.

She and Weston lived over the gas station and I used to eat supper with them at least three times a week. Wes was something: handsome, though his face was always stubbly and his hands were always dirty even if he washed them. I wondered if Della minded him touching her body with those grubby fingers— like when I was a kid and used to wonder about how

Mrs. Walocek, the fishmonger's wife, felt. Mr. Walocek was always smiling, he didn't seem unloved, and once I asked Mom about it. She didn't know what I was talking about, so I explained about his being up to his elbows in carp and mackerel all day long and how the smell must be indelible. Mom was embarrassed and blushed and shrugged and said, "Leda July, there's more to love than that."

Than what? I wondered, but by then I was afraid to ask. More to it than sex or more to it than what your partner smells like? I continued to wonder about these things and about the Waloceks' love life. If Mrs. Walocek could love him in spite of his smelly hands, there was either something wonderful about Mr. Walocek that didn't show or something about love I didn't know.

I wondered about Wes and Della, too. It seemed that Della was always laughing at home and falling into Wes's lap, and he was always chasing her into the living room, where he'd tackle her on the green couch. Always laughing. Mom and Daddy never laughed, so I didn't wonder much about them. Now I wonder why they never laughed.

You couldn't really say my folks were unhappy—they never complained and were always counting their blessings—but they hardly ever smiled. Mom's usually waxen face had a cute little habit of winking one eye when she was feeling feisty, but that was about it. Still, all my friends thought my parents were great because they didn't fight with each other or punish me and there were always home-baked goodies after school. And you couldn't find cleaner hands than on my Daddy. They always smelled of soap. We were sort of like the perfect family, so everyone was shocked when I ran away.

Things were going along okay at Rosie's. I made good tips—nothing spectacular but enough to keep me in art supplies and feeling pretty proud of making my way alone. The holidays were busy, with everybody in town all day and into the evening to do their Christmas shopping. People were more generous, too. I made enough in two weeks to get a small set of oil paints, some turp, and a canvas, and I set out to do my first oil painting since high school. I decided to paint a portrait of Della and Wes for their Christmas present. They'd been great to me—like parents, only better—in between best friends and parents. When I told them about the picture they were thrilled. Della said she was honored and Wes said, "Well, June-bird,"—that's what he called me, don't ask me why—

"make me look like Elvis, now, you hear?" He was kidding, I hope, because he was more handsome than Elvis by a mile.

Sunday morning when I went to Della and Wes's, they were all decked out in their church clothes, ready to pose for me. I'd never even seen them dressed like that and to tell the truth, it was sort of strange. They sat on the green couch and we put the vase of plastic daisies on the table next to them for composition, and on the other side Flapper, their old cocker spaniel, lay at Wes's feet. Della never looked prettier, except her face looked sort of frightened. There was almost a holy feeling in that room, as if they really were in church and posing for God Himself. And I tell you, maybe God *was* there in the room, because later, while doing my painting, I felt something I don't think I'll ever forget.

To begin with, there was that look on Della's face, and the feeling in the room that I just chalked up to them never having had their picture painted. But soon I began to wonder, where'd the real Della go, the one who came into Rosie's for doughnuts, laughing and teasing Al about his beer belly? Or was this the real Della? I sort of wanted to ask her about it, but it was hard to know how. Then I looked at Wes, his chin as

smooth as a girl's. I'd never even *seen* his chin. He
looked like a movie star, and real serious, which
seemed like an awful strain on his face—as if something right below the surface wanted to burst out
howling and slap Della on the butt.

Right after I started to paint, Wes began to shift
and twitch uncomfortably, but Della was amazing. I
swear that girl didn't move a hair for one half-hour
except for nudging Wes to keep still. And then, when
I put down my brush and said let's take a break, she
still didn't move until Wes leaned over and tickled her.
After a few reluctant giggles she was back to normal.

We worked till four o'clock and then Wes brought
out a six-pack. He guzzled about one and a half beers
right down and the old Wes sprung out from his face.
I could almost see the whiskers pop off his chin. Della
changed into her slinky pink tricot top that con-
formed to all her curves, and lay down on the couch
swilling a Bud. Everything was back to normal. The
partially finished portrait with its somber faces stood
in the corner watching us all like the parents in the
back of a girl's mind when she kisses a guy for the
first time.

That was the night Weston asked me if I was a vir-
gin, which of course I was, but I didn't tell *him*.

It was hard to wait all week to get back to my portrait but we were all working different days and the light wasn't right at night. It wasn't so great at Rosie's these days. It only takes a couple of grouchy customers to ruin your whole shift. "The pie ain't hot enough," "This toast tastes like charcoal,"—fine, but they get so pissed off about it, as if you just served them up their own guts on a platter. And even if you reheat the pie and smile and say, "Sorry, this should be nice and tasty for you" or something like that, they don't tip you and they don't forgive you, even if you give them á la mode for free.

Sunday finally came and Della made banana pancakes before we got down to work. She was laughing as she went to the bedroom to change into her white dress but the minute she sat down her face fell, her eyes glazed over, she was like a statue—I tell you she hardly blinked. Wes, too, sat sober as a judge and I just stared at them for a minute, at their unfamiliar faces. What's with these expressions? I thought. It's like I'd suddenly been transported into someone else's living room where I didn't know anyone. It felt sort of like the "Twilight Zone" and I imagined that if I talked to them as Della and Wes they might not know who I was or what I was talking about. I blinked and picked up my brush, but I couldn't paint. I looked back at Della. I wanted to say something, anything, like, "Hi, Della," but that seemed like a pretty stupid thing to say in the middle of nothing so I clammed up. I clammed up tighter and tighter till I thought I would explode. What could I say? I didn't know quite how to explain to them that they looked like two aliens from another time zone.

"Smile," I finally managed to say. But they didn't. They were too uptight. They look like my parents, I said to myself, and they really did. And then it came to me. That was when I first realized that my parents too were only pretending to be like my parents. I should never have thought this, I guess, for that strange thought widened out in my brain like an angry river. Who were Bill and Edna, really? And then again, who was I?

For the first time since I had left I felt pretty far from home. Not that I wanted to go back; well, maybe a little, but if I did I wanted to find Mom laughing like Della usually did and hugging me and I knew she'd just wink and say, "I baked you some brownies, Leda July." There was no place to go. There was no such place as home anymore and my whole sixteen years of life collapsed in my lap. I looked at my paints. How was I supposed to make these blobs of color into something resembling a human being? What had given me the feeling that I could be an artist in the first place? Was that what I was pretending to be? Sweet Jesus, I was just a little girl in a world that didn't differentiate me from any of a zillion blades of grass. God! I screamed inside as Wes and Della continued to sit politely on the couch, unaware of the earthquake that had just struck me. I screamed where only I could hear the screaming. I wanted to cry out, "Mama!" but it was God I called on. I guess God is for when you know there's no point calling for your mama. So what if He can't answer back or comfort you in normal ways. You know He's listening.

I put my brushes on the table and sat down, trying to steady my brain. It was just like I'd read at the beginning of *The Bhagavad-Gita* when Arjuna gets so dizzy he feels like he can't fight his battle. And this was my battle with Bill and Edna.

I looked back at Wes and Della, who weren't Wes and Della, and strange ideas rushed into my mind. What might Mom have been if she'd ever stopped pretending? Or Daddy? And anyway, how'd they pick those two people to pretend to be? It seemed to me that as long as you were pretending, you might as well pretend to be some heavy dude—what's to stop you from pretending to be Gaugin or Herman Hesse or Madame Curie? Why Edna Ruskin? If you're only pretending anyway, why should you be limited by your talents, or by anything? How come even in the world of lies, you're limited by the truth?

"Smile, Della," I said again, and it felt like it took all my strength to say it.

"Why?" she asked, trying scrupulously not to move her lips.

"I'd like to capture the real you," I answered. "You know, your personality." I tried to sound calm but my voice felt like a little boat on a wild sea.

Della eked out a grin and I said, "That's better." But it wasn't much.

I was trying to pull myself together, to focus on the work. My eyes moved slowly over Wes's strong hands, his broad chest, his smooth jaw. He looked really cool. It seems off, but I don't believe I ever saw Daddy with even the first stubble of a beard until I was twelve years old, and when one morning I did, I turned my head away. It was like I had seen him naked. Should I use a warm crimson to shade Della's cheek or a cool cerulean blue? I sat there holding the brush. Mom's hairdo never changed in sixteen years.

She pinned it up in a tight French twist at the back of her head, with fringy bangs in the front. Della's hair hung to her shoulders and the light fell through it like a waterfall.

I must have worked for almost an hour. I stood back to see what I had done and was surprised, for the picture looked more alive than the people sitting in front of me. The real Della was still reluctant to move although I could see her inconspicuously wiggling her feet, which must have been good and asleep by now.

"Time for a break?" Wes asked, noticing I'd stopped painting. I nodded, my throat too dry to talk.

I collapsed in a nearby armchair. Wes came over and stood behind me to look at the portrait. "Hey!" he said with astonishment, leaning in to take a closer look. I could feel the warmth of his skin through his shirt. It leaped the gap between us, and I could smell him. The unimaginably sweet smell of cologne heated by clean perspiration made me even dizzier than I already was, nauseated by the mixture of emotions and sensations. When Wes walked away I sat back, sighed an uneven sigh, and closed my eyes.

I heard Della say she was going to lay her aching body down in the bedroom for a while, and Wes stretched out on the carpet. I couldn't believe what was going on in my mind. I wanted to say something to someone, but I felt like I couldn't talk at all, so I just squeezed my eyes tight as if that would shut out the images that raced through my brain. It didn't, and I was treated to the picture of Gunther Graves's face, his bestial crotch, and the way he leered as he lunged at me. I felt far more scared now than I had when it actually happened. Odd, I thought, as if the memory were more real than the event itself. He wasn't even here. All that was here now was my own mind, which had turned some kind of dark corner behind which marched an endless parade of frightening faces.

I opened my eyes and saw Della smiling at me, a big juicy smile like the first time I'd seen her come bouncing into Rosie's. But it wasn't Della, it was my painting. And there was Wes, big as life, sitting with his arm around her, his skin almost pulsing with a ruddy glow. I could hardly believe I had painted it.

"It's done," I said quietly. "It's done."

"Well, all right then! Let's party!" Wes hollered, jumping up from the floor. This time he brought out some Tequila and took a slug right from the bottle. "Whoo!" he exhaled as if he were on fire, then poured me a glassful of the stuff.

Della shuffled in from the bedroom. "What's going on in here?" she asked sleepily.

"We're celebratin', baby," Wes said, grabbing her buns. "Our own little Rembrandt has finished immortalizing us." He poured her a glass as she came around to look at the picture. She just clapped her hands and kissed my cheek. She didn't say a thing until Wes handed her the glass. Then, holding it up to the sky, she said, "To Leda July, to art, to—"

"Oh, hell, Della, drink it down!" Wes said. She did, but first she said, "To friendship!"

I just sat there eyeing my glass.

"You too, June-bird," he said. "Go ahead. You look like you could use a drink."

I guess I must have looked pretty weird. I still felt pretty weird. I took a sip and it tasted foul. I smiled like a coward but I took another little sip. Since it still tasted like something you'd want to wash the floors with that would stink up the house for a whole day, I set it down. Wes laughed and put his hand on my shoulder. There was magic in that hand. First of all it seemed to cover my whole back, or maybe it was just the warmth from it spreading all up my neck, out my arms and down my spine. Then he put on some really hot salsa music and asked me to dance.

"I can't dance," I said as he grabbed my hand and pulled me off the chair, dancing me around the room. I laughed while he was whirling me and my head began to spin again. But this time it was more like fun. His stained hands definitely were much bigger than I would have thought, and they felt dry and warm. I breathed him in from the wind we created around us as we danced and I could smell that sweaty but sweet essence of Wes. Like a kid searching for the brass ring on a merry-go-round, I kept catching a look at Della's face as we swung around—she was sitting back with an open-mouthed grin, just enjoying us enjoying ourselves. And then I'd get a glimpse of the painting, smiling along with us. It made me laugh and I laughed and laughed till we were all laughing.

"I think I might throw up," I said. Wes let up pretty quickly after that. I flopped into the chair and was okay once I sat down. In fact, looking out across the room, I felt like I had a clear blue ocean flowing in my blood and I had just set sail for Tahiti.

The Clock

It started to become evident that I wasn't going to see him again, so what was the point of remembering his name? I must admit, now that I've forgotten it, there are times I wish I could remember and turn it over on my tongue just for the fun of it. After all this time it gets hard . . . how long has it been? My friends used to say, "Forget him," and I tried, I really did, but I couldn't. Now I can't remember what it was I couldn't forget. It's difficult to think. The labored hum of the electric clock distracts me. There's something wrong with it, it never had to work so hard before, as if single-handedly it had to bring forth time. I don't like the sound of it, it's threatening to break down, although it will probably outlast me with its menacing wheeze. I remember Sanford once said, "No one likes to be threatened"—Sanford? Was that it? I don't know, but I think that's what he said. Not much of a thought, is it? Although maybe it's a question of context, of which I have none at the moment.

In all this confusion, little things do come back to me. Like the time he fixed his eyes on me and said, "I'm afraid I am capable of breaking your heart." It nearly broke his heart to say it, you could see it on his face, which also appeared to be breaking. Maybe that's what happened to him. Maybe he broke and I had to throw him out—like the clock—for I suppose I'll have to throw it out if it ever actually breaks.

I relied on that clock once. I took it totally for granted, too, until one day something happened that forced me to take notice of my clock's existence. As I recall, it began running just a little bit fast, and then a little faster still, and over the months proceeded to keep decreasingly accurate time. At first I would correct the five-, and later the ten-minute discrepancy, but after a while I grew so accustomed to its quirky rhythm, its inexplicable rush into the future, that I simply made the adjustment in my head, easily and naturally allowing for its small margin of error. If it said five o'clock, I'd say to myself, "Ah yes, it's five of five." And then later as it raced further ahead of itself I'd say, "Yes, yes, ten of five." I was satisfied to proceed in this manner, perhaps too satisfied, for it never occurred to me that maybe I was taking on more than my share of the responsibility for keeping time. As far as I was concerned, this was just the way things worked between me and my clock. Unfortunately, I had failed to consider the factor of the cumulative error. Besides, I was too stubborn or otherwise unwilling to make the fast-encroaching fifteen-minute adjustment. Looking back on it now that it is, so to speak, too late, it is probably more accurate to say that I was constitutionally unable to go beyond that ten-minute correction. It seemed so petty not to give my clock just five more minutes of the benefit of my doubts, and yet where would it end? At any rate, I simply could not bring myself to say eleven-fifteen when it so clearly said eleven-thirty. In my mind that was no longer an adjustment, that would have been a blatant lie. Whether it was my lie or the clock's was not totally clear, so I stuck to my pristine ten-minute emendation of the facts.

I do not mean to imply that any of this was conscious belligerence on my part, I am merely pointing out the limits of my adaptability. I couldn't go any further, I simply couldn't. Instead, I plodded along naively with the ten-minute compromise after it had long since become asynchronous. In time, slowly, against my will and without my knowledge, I became an anachronism in my own life, for while I had stopped at ten minutes, my clock would stop at nothing. Fifteen minutes was nowhere near the end of my clock's distortions; it was just the beginning.

It all seems so trivial and at some point perhaps it was, but right now, to be honest, I don't have the slightest idea what time it is. I look at my clock, ticking innocently if somewhat noisily along, and its face is a mendacious blank. Its hands indicate half past twelve but I don't begin to know what that means. It could mean anything, absolutely anything, perhaps even half past twelve. We are in different worlds, maybe different time zones; there is a complete lack of trust in any information it imparts. We merely co-exist.

There have been times when I have thought to myself, What the hell, why not just pull the plug and forget about the damn clock—get a new clock; it's not doing you any good as it is. On the contrary, it makes matters worse by giving you the impression that you know what time it is, when in fact the clock has a life of its own that doesn't intersect with your or anyone else's idea of what time it is. But I don't do it, I don't pull the plug, I don't know why. To be sure, it's a nice clock with large, readable numbers and a pretty blue face, but that hardly seems reason enough to go on living like this.

I venture to say it was not always like this. Now that I think about it, I can remember the terrible shock when I first awoke to the situation, and I vaguely recall that he—whoever he was—was no help. It was sudden, as sudden as it now becomes so vivid in my mind. I remember the day as if it were yesterday. It is so vivid, in fact, that it brings back the days when I knew precisely how long ago yesterday was.

Life was simpler then, and I awoke bright and early one morning to the eager ring of the clock. How I used to love that ring, not a jangle or a cranky buzz but a clear, sweet jingle inviting me to the possibilities of a new day. I rolled over and turned it off, stretched luxuriously, and arose to get ready for work. I left the house as always, with a bounce in my step; it was cold and crisp outside, and I walked happily the twenty blocks to my office. Only as I neared the tall marble building where I worked did I have any suspicion that something was wrong. Then, for reasons I could not understand, it began to get dark. I thought perhaps it was going to rain, but there was not a cloud in the sky. The other people on the street didn't seem the least bit disturbed by this strange turn of events. This actually proved to be somewhat reassuring at first, like being on a turbulent airplane when your fears are allayed by the sight of all the other passengers, undisturbed, eating their Chicken Kiev. But on this odd gray morning I was not reassured for long by the sanguine attitudes of passersby, and considered instead that there must be something wrong with *them*. They were probably in a gray fog themselves, oblivious to the world around them. How superior I felt, but secretly, how scared.

I decided to continue on with my day—what else could I do?—and I waited patiently by the elevators, all of which arrived at the ground floor full of people. I rode up alone except for one little man, his head cast toward the ground, cap pulled over his eyes. Although clearly inviting me not to speak, I said casually, "Strange morning, don't you think?" Then I wondered aloud why everyone was leaving the building.

As soon as I said it panic struck. Of course! There must be some kind of bomb threat! And I might be sharing an elevator with the very man for whom police could at that moment be searching. The law firm for which I am employed is on the fifty-ninth floor. We were on the twentieth. By the thirty-first I realized that a bomb threat would answer the latter part of my question but wouldn't explain the precipitously dark sky.

"It's almost six o'clock," the man said, flashing me a suspicious glance, clearly more afraid of me than I was of him.

"A.M. or P.M.?" I asked tentatively, but at that moment the doors opened and he disappeared. When I stepped out at my floor and entered our suite of offices, the only one there was the janitor.

"Good morning, John," I said (still not quite able to admit the obvious). "Where is everyone?"

"They're all gone for the day, miss."

"Yes, of course," I said knowingly, and by then I *did* know, for looking out the window I saw the sun disappearing in the western sky.

I hung up my coat and looked around. The room was tired with the fatigue of an office at day's end, wastebaskets filled, the smell of stale perfume, the buzz of activity lingering in the air. I sat at my desk and glanced at the intercom, thankful at least that I wouldn't be bothered by Mr. Holt's constant demands . . . until I saw his memo.

"Please type these reports to the state prosecutor ASAP. We will discuss your attendance when you return. It won't do to disappear like this without notice, and while you have kept up admirably with your work, your constant tardiness is becoming an inconvenience to the firm. J.H."

I worked through the night to type up those reports, and when I finally looked up, stretching to get the kink out of my neck, the other secretaries were arriving for work. Mona stood before me with her smiling face and said cheerfully, "Well, you're here bright and early for a change." I muttered something about how nice it is to get an early start, and grabbing my coat I left, without looking back, hoping not to run into Mr. Holt.

I made it down to the elevator and out onto the street and didn't stop running till I got home. As I collapsed in the chair the phone rang. It was Stan . . . Sal? Sylvester? At any rate, "he" was in an uncharacteristic fury. It seems that not only had I missed (or rather misplaced) my day at the office, I had worked all the way through our dinner date. I was shocked to find how unyielding he was about matters of time. Furthermore, he who had always been so reasonable and loving had assumed some kind of malicious intent on my part. I quickly explained what had happened: "I overslept," I said. "My clock has not been working well, as you know." I felt sure he'd understand. "It can happen to anyone," I expected him to say.

I was not yet fully aware of his obsession with punctuality, how precise he was, exacting and fanatical about time. But it seems my clock, with its casual approach, had rendered us utterly incompatible. Things were never the same after that. He could no longer really trust that I would be where I said I'd be when I said I'd be there, and frankly, I could not in good faith assure him that I would. If a simple rendezvous was problematic, any deeper communion was clearly out of the question. He had not yet accepted the seriousness of the situation and attempted to rescue the remains of our relationship with what he thought was a simple solution. "You'd better just throw out that old clock," he said.

"Throw it out? My clock? Why?" I inquired, feeling his suggestion to be a bit extreme.

"Just throw it out. You'll get a nice new clock. I'll buy you one myself," he offered. "Digital."

At that I panicked. His life was so strict, his demands so stringent. If he said 10:15, this man did not mean 10:14, he did not mean 10:16. After all this time spent in relative timelessness, could I adjust to the rigors of his digital living? In the end I kept the clock, and as I suspected earlier, I threw him out.

The Storybook

Sometimes my life feels very small, as if it could fit in a tiny cottage in a child's picture book—one of those cozy cottages that a little girl wanders away from one morning while a pretty lady in an apron waves to her from the front door, and the girl gets in all sorts of trouble before the book ends. That's how small I feel, as if my life is turning within the pages of a storybook, and whoever is waving good-bye to me is just about two inches tall. As I walk away, I shiver and my face contorts with fear. I know this because I hear the voice of a man reading the little book. Who is he, I wonder? He reads aloud to someone, I gather: He's too old to be reading such a book by himself. Well, if he says my face is contorted with fear, I guess my face is contorted with fear, and as soon as I hear him say it I try to straighten out my face—I wouldn't want everyone looking at me with a screwed-up face—and by the time he turns the page, I'm whistling. He thinks it's because of my courage when it's really shame or vanity. So I get smashed between the preceding pages, whistling when I don't feel like whistling, and there I stay frozen till someone else decides to read the book.

I have no idea who wrote this book. And as I say, I have no idea who's reading it. Whoever he is, he spots a little bird flying around my house. He says it's following me now: "There's a little bluebird following the girl," he says, and I look up and sure enough, there's the little bird. "Well, whaddaya know," I say, but I guess he doesn't hear me because he doesn't say that I said it. Ah, but now I see that it must be a little girl he's reading to because I hear her ask my name. "Sandy," he tells her, except that my name is Lila.

Night falls on the next page—yellow six-pointed stars on a dark blue background, and a full moon with a face on it. It may not sound so bad, but I'm alone here, and I'm scared shitless and the man doesn't say a word about that. Either doesn't notice or he doesn't care and all he says is that I stop by the great oak tree for the night and cuddle up in the light of the big round moon. Moonlight nothing, it's black as pitch out here and I honestly don't know if I can hang on till the next page. I feel so alone, I'm losing it now—I begin to hallucinate, nothing seems real, it's as if the trees are made of cardboard and maybe I am, too, and the dew is like ashes. There's no one human in the whole wide world and even the little girl he's reading to has fallen fast asleep.

"Myrtle! Myrtle!" All of a sudden I hear the woman in the apron calling from way, way back at the cottage, using whatever literary devices she can muster to traverse the miles and the pages. Myrtle? Who's Myrtle? The man said my name was Sandy, and although it isn't, it certainly isn't Myrtle. Wait a minute, maybe this isn't even my story. Maybe I've accidentally wandered into someone else's story entirely. And if he isn't narrating *my* life, perhaps I'm just a part of his, one story from his past, one moment from a headful of memories swarming in his mind as he reads his little girl her book. Book? What book? Maybe there is no book at all and whoever Myrtle is or isn't is no business of mine. Perhaps these are all just transient thoughts that occupy him as he makes his way through the day. He could be reading *Goldilocks and the Three Bears* for all I know; I could be just an undercurrent of silent chemicals coursing through his blood. Still, if he *is* the author of my life, whose book is *he* in? Does he know he's being read by me?

Actors and Sam

Everybody was acting like somebody else. The butcher was acting like his brother, the CPA; the CPA was acting like his father, the fishmonger, who was dead. The fishmonger's widow was acting like a sultry singer half her age and weight, and the sultry singer was acting like Marilyn Monroe who was dead.

On television and in movies people were acting like rapists, housewives, and rapscallions. Kids were acting like millionaires and millionaires were acting out megalomaniacal fantasies.

Movie stars were acting like movie stars. Yuppies were acting as if death were only in the movies and acting as if they were *in* these movies. Impoverished Blacks and Hispanics were acting as if society were halfway tolerable and the upper middle classes were doing a convincing job of acting as if life in the twentieth century were worth living.

There was one man who was not acting like anyone. When he took a walk he felt the sun on his head. His name was Sam. He walked slowly, sometimes fast. He smiled at passersby and said, "Good morning," or he didn't. He sold books in a bookstore and gave his honest opinion about the books. "It's good," he said. "I liked it." He called one customer a pain in the ass for accusing him of being slow on the register. He sat and ate his lunch in the park. He gave Fritos to the birds. He wished he could have an ice cream but he couldn't digest lactose. He felt his skin scream when a redhead went by in a short skirt, even though he was married and old enough to be her father. He loved a good laugh but all too rarely had one. He sometimes thought he was an eagle or a sparrow. He always looked forward expectantly to seeing his wife when he went home after work, though sometimes it didn't live up to his expectations.

No one had really noticed that Sam was not acting. They just thought he was a little strange. The way he seemed so intent upon not missing a moment of life, though life often made him nauseous. The way he let people see him feel in public. The way he really seemed to believe that someday he would die and that his life on earth was as important as a blade of grass, the way he never prayed in conventional ways—in silence or in private—but while he was talking to you or eating Saltines or paying for toothpaste. The way he prayed, eyes on the sun, though he was in the storeroom sorting Michelin guides. The way he said, "Thank you," like he meant it, "Coke, please," like he meant it, and "I hope you have a nice vacation," like he meant it. The way he couldn't help meaning things as much as the best actors tried to mean things, but never would because they were acting.

Louie Hoped

The main word in Louie's vocabulary was *if,* and he abused it day and night. He was tired of hoping though and hoped to God that one day his prayers would be answered so he could stop hoping so hard. No one hoped quite so hard as Louie, but then no one had quite so little hope as he did—no job, no money, no family, no pets. His fondest hope was to have all his hopes fulfilled and so be left to enjoy the fruits of all his scrupulous hoping.

Technically, Louie was no dope. He knew that total realization was, for hopes, totally hopeless, so he set his sights more conservatively on the hope that one day he would be cured of such dopey hoping. He'd had a glimpse of those clear blue skies on several occasions in the form of promising (and hopeful) relationships, like the one with Nannette, but these he'd always treated like a storm, something to be gotten in out of. He'd battened down his hatches, never before having even known that he owned any hatches, but found in those trying times that he had hatches all over the place. Where he'd learned to batten so well he did not know, but once he got started it was clear that he had had experience in this area. He wondered if he'd worked as a hatch battener in a previous lifetime at sea. He'd never before had the inclination to muse about the past, so occupied was he hoping for the future, but soon Louie found himself spending most of his time musing (and battening) when he wasn't, of course, hoping.

Life was full. Louie still had nothing, but the possibilities of time upon which he mused filled him with a kind of hope he'd never before even hoped to hope for. It was, to begin with, infinite, and it didn't end there. It was confusing, though, and not altogether pleasant, for it introduced a level of existence he could only vaguely sense, and if there was one thing Louie hated it was things that could barely be sensed. It was one of the reasons he hated having to hope so hard in the first place, for hoping always engaged the vague future of your most private desires. Louie was in for it. His new sense of hope was dangerous and threatened to rip up all his carefully battened hatches. Poor Louie could do nothing but sit down and hope that soon it would all end.

It didn't. The past and the future seemed to meet in his brain. He felt the fluid nonsense of watery thoughts and feared he would drown, having been too busy hoping as a child to have learned how to swim. He turned against his own hopes, blaming them for his failure to meet them, and he even lost sight of what to hope for. The kind of global hoping in which he'd always engaged was obviously inadequate to the task. It was clear that he'd have to find more specific hopes to hope for and then hope to attain them, but he felt so little hope of finding them in the first place.

By now Louie was almost totally hopeless, and was discovered there by Nannette, still hoping but at the end of his rope. She approached him where he sat, slouched over on his couch, and tenderly touched his hand. It was just a touch, but in that touch Louie felt a fire in his mind that burned and seared, leaving him completely without hope and yet, strangely, not exactly hopeless. He felt naked and took off his clothes. Nannette followed suit with her dress and for the first time in his life, Louie was not hoping for anything else.

The Big Bang

Lucy almost died giving birth to an orgasm for which she had been waiting for years. She'd had plenty of others along the way but this one with James was The One without which she knew she never could have rested in peace. It shook her to the beginning of her soul and beyond, unearthing deeply buried portions of time, some of which weren't even hers. Several Napoleonic wars marched across her mental landscape as they made their way through the universal mind—battles, victories and defeats, stately parades down the Champs-Elysées, and a discussion with Josephine about silverware. Lucy tried to shake off these notable and irrelevant historical moments, but when she did they were simply replaced by more mundane scenarios from the cosmic unconscious. This differed somewhat from the collective unconscious which had collected its memories for some greater purpose.

In these ordinary visions there was no purpose, greater or otherwise, no mythological design; they were just things that had happened. There was no reason for anyone to think them anymore, but once in a while a really tremendous orgasm like Lucy's jarred these things loose from the garbage bin of human events. She was soon privy to a squash game between Mick Bradley (who'd invented the first car cigarette lighter but failed to get a patent) and his old barber, George. George lost. Back and forth they volleyed in Lucy's head till she screamed, "Stop! Stop!" But of course they didn't, not until the game was over.

She was totally powerless over this realm of time unraveling. Eventually the volleying stopped and though George did challenge Mick to a rematch, thank God for Lucy's sake, Mick was smart enough to quit while he was ahead. Sweaty and exhausted, they went out for a couple of beers, which wasn't so bad except that George smoked cigars and Lucy began to choke. She held her breath, hoping that George and Mick would soon slip back into the wave that space-time had burped up in her face. She couldn't be stuck with these two clowns forever—she had after all managed safely to escape the Napoleonic Wars—but Mick Bradley and his barber George proved more tenacious than the little emperor had been, and she was stuck with them for days. She switched back and forth between their two lives, which dovetailed daily on the squash court of her brain.

Lucy's head ached, for at night George beat his wife. Lucy found some relief at the barber shop watching fat men get shaved and shampooed, but this was small consolation for the pain of having her own life take a backseat to the brutalizing certainty of living time that had already been lived by someone else. The outcomes of George's and Mick's lives were clear and the events leading up to them seemed somehow to know this; they were intractable and boring to watch. She'd almost rather have gone back to Napoleon, whose furniture at least was much more attractive, but the choice was not hers. It wasn't even Mick's or George's, whose petty lives, she realized, were doomed to be replayed indefinitely—if not in her mind then in someone else's or in the void of used-up time. As she considered the facts, she began to have sympathy for these men and for the rest of humanity, who were all victims of fate. With the appearance of such merciful thoughts, Lucy felt

George and Mick miraculously release from her brain, once more rejoining the cosmic gases from which they had emerged. Her own mind rejoined itself in the present.

She felt James heavy on top of her and smiled. He rolled off as she shifted her weight, then he snuggled up against her. Lucy kissed his forehead and he awoke with a sleepy grin.

"Oh, I must have dozed off," he said. "Weird little dream. God, I haven't thought about that guy for years."

"Who?" Lucy asked.

"From my home town—George, the barber. He owned a shop right in the middle of town. We'd go and watch him give haircuts on Saturday nights," James laughed.

"George?" Lucy asked, stunned, a mild panic in her eyes.

"Yeah, he used to hang around with this crazy inventor, shoot, what was his name—"

"Mick," Lucy offered.

"Christ Almighty, Lucy, how'd you guess *that*?"

Silently she stared at James, unable to answer.

"Come on, baby," he pressured, "how in the world did you guess old Mick Fielding's name?"

"Fielding? Wait a minute, I thought his name was Bradley," she said, confused.

"Why would you think that? Why the hell would you think anything about Mick Fielding?" he asked, as confused as she. "Have you been talking to my dad?"

Lucy couldn't explain it herself, of course, and the word *cosmic* was not one that James liked to hear first thing in the morning.

"I think I may have tapped into your dream," Lucy ventured tentatively. For some reason James found this to be an acceptable explanation, and although he looked somewhat queasy for the rest of the day, he never brought it up again. Lucy could not be quite so sanguine, for there were so many questions still left unanswered. Who was Mick Bradley? And how did Napoleon fit into all of this? It worried her to think about other chapters of history still unread, and to ponder those too ghastly to reread with such immediacy. For now she would have to live with the fact that when the earth moved there were dangers, apparently, of the sky opening as well.

Nietzsche Speaks

Give Frances a little too much to drink and the transformation was astounding. Something happened to her that was uncanny, a paradox inexplicable to the experts of medical science. Given a few belts of whiskey, this wild-spirited young woman—who was known when stone-cold sober to jump naked into public fountains—became utterly and incontrovertibly conventional, with a sudden talent for deep philosophical thought. No one could explain it, least of all Frances, who remembered almost nothing of these temporary bouts of sanity. After a sordid night of boozing, Frances would come home in her version of a drunken stupor and hungrily devour *Ecce Homo* or *The Will to Power*, writing long essays on Nietzsche that were published in serious journals of philosophy. She soon carved out quite a little niche for herself as a Nietzsche scholar, and her work became widely respected in the halls of academe.

Frances's life was was grossly complicated by her success as a philosopher. For one thing, in her uninebriated state she was a beautician who didn't understand one word of what she had written when drunk. This gave life an eerie schizoid quality, and made editing out of the question. She was aware of her altered state, but just barely, and it bore no connection to the ditzy broad she was generally known to be.

The real trouble started, however, one Monday morning when Frances, late for work, was leaving for the salon. The phone rang and it was yet another offer, with a hefty advance, to do a book on the life and work of Friedrich Nietzsche. For some reason, this time she accepted—too rushed perhaps to come up with an excuse quickly enough to extricate herself from this embarrassing situation. It was always difficult to explain that what they'd taken for genius were the loose ramblings of a drunken hairdresser, and who can say, maybe Frances had finally started to believe in herself.

Frances made a date for a lunch meeting with the publisher of Parthenon Press, without a clue as to what she would do once she got there. But it was better than facing another cold turkey sandwich between perms, and anyway, she thought she might enjoy being a famous Nietzsche scholar for a change, meet some new people, have a little caviar and champagne. She *had* written the stuff, after all, even though most of it sounded like Greek to her.

To make a long story short, Mr. Parthenon Press was gorgeous and Frances fell in love. It was like a dream come true, for he seemed to like her, too, and was not put off by her fishnet stockings or her ratted maroon hair. He was not even put off by her squeaky nasal voice, and he actually seemed charmed to think that someone who looked and sounded like a dumb floozy could have such a rare mind. But mainly, lucky for her, he got her drunk. Such fine champagne in such abundance! And when she got really sloppy she started quoting Schopenhauer. She spoke of his early influence on Nietzsche's thought and elucidated masterfully their divergent attitudes on the question of will.

Mr. Parthenon Press was fascinated all the way through to his underwear and hoped to get her brains into bed that night. In her current state, Frances was too involved with Nietzsche to care much about anything else, but fortunately she had sobered up by the time they reached her escort's apartment and she fell willingly into his arms.

Upon awakening next morning, Frances luxuriated in the memories of the previous night, her body still quivering. Once again her future publisher unwittingly made passionate love to a woman without a thought in her head. At breakfast he finally proposed the contract for a new Nietzsche tome, and after some hesitation Frances shrugged and said, "Sure, I'll take a crack at it." He looked at her a bit askance, then laughed at the charming earthiness of her ways, so refreshing after the intellectual stiffs he usually had to deal with.

He requested an outline, including some biographical information about Nietzsche's relationship with his sister. Was Elizabeth Nietzsche merely protective of her brilliant brother's work, he queried, or baldly ambitious, possessive, seeking gain and glory only for herself?

"I dunno," Frances said, slathering her roll with strawberry jam and lunging at it as if it might escape her mouth. He rephrased the question. Frances began to get uncomfortable and lost her appetite. She sat back with a sullen sigh, and he asked worriedly what was wrong.

"I dunno, I feel a little sick. It musta been all that fancy champagne," she said, thinking fast.

For the moment her host forgot all about Nietzsche as the warm memory of their passion flooded through his blood. He looked at her with concern and lust and asked if there was anything he could do.

"Yeah, stop talkin' about this Nietzsche guy, will ya? Ya make me feel like a whore, like ya only like me for my mind or somethin'."

"Oh no," he said, taking her soft white hand, spiked with its long, red, sculptured nails. "I assure you I am not interested in you only for your mind."

"You're just sayin' that," she whined.

"No, no, really, it's true."

"What if I didn't know a thing about this Nietzsche guy, huh?" she challenged. "Then what? It would be good-bye Frances, that's what."

"Not at all, my dear. What I find charming about you is that your fascinating mind is so natural. It just augments your beauty and appeal."

"Gee, thanks," she said, glowing again and forgetting she was dumb as an ox. When he steered the conversation back to business, however, she was once again at a loss as to how to respond. Luckily he offered her some brandy for her coffee. Skipping the coffee, she slugged down a whole cupful.

After that he couldn't have stopped her if he'd

tried. Frances, bursting with ideas, could barely contain her rage at "that Nietzsche bitch with her conniving, fascist, gold-digging lies." Once again enraptured and now hopelessly enchanted by her coy cat-and-mouse intellect, Mr. Parthenon Press right then and there gave her a contract and a $50,000 advance for a two-volume work on the great philosopher.

"Gee, thanks," she said.

Of course, there was no way she could live up to his belief in her, short of becoming an alcoholic, and so, drunk day and night, Frances produced reams of brilliant and original discourse. By now a serious lush, she lost her job at the beauty parlor but made the deadline with time to burn. Proudly, and to much foofaraw from the publishing world, she watched her book enter the public domain. It was so well received that they offered her another book focusing solely on *Thus Spoke Zarathustra*.

"Thus spoke *who*?" she asked. But she'd had enough. Her mind was so marinated that she no longer knew who she was. She'd lost her job, her friends, and everything that made any sense to her. If this is what it meant to be smart, she wanted none of it. She was tired of being smart, of being sober when she was drunk, and of never having any fun. But it wasn't so simple giving it all up; it meant losing Mr. Parthenon Press as well. When she finally faced up to who she really was, she had to leave him, and he was devastated, too.

Frances sat alone night after night, a dumb unemployed beautician/Nietzsche scholar, crying in misery, bereft—and she didn't even know what that meant. She cursed the book she had written and threw it across the room. It landed with a thud near her sleeping cat, who awoke with a howl and went screaming from the house. The silence that had enveloped her for days was broken.

Frances felt better for her outburst. She eyed the book with suspicion, she picked it up again and wondered what it said. She yearned for a drink, but knowing where that led, simply sat quietly with the book in her lap.

There it was—Frances Powers—her God-given name big as life right there on the cover. People seemed to think it was really something, this book, and she felt proud. With great ceremony, she opened to the first page.

"Dialectic? What the hell's a dialectic, for Christ's sake? And who the hell's this Zarathustra?"

She dropped the book as if it were burning her

hand and cursed the devil, it must have been the devil's work. Her mind was a blur, she felt dizzy, she felt ill, she felt drunk—or at least what most people felt when they were drunk—plastered, sloshed, blotto, though she hadn't touched a drop.

Staggering around the room and bumping into furniture, she shouted at the damnable book, calling it names and beseeching God to cast out the evil from her soul. Her chest was heaving, her heart about to burst, she felt trapped. If she did not read the book it would destroy her, she knew this, and so once more she forced herself to read.

The words dripped and swam before her eyes like frantic spermatozoa, they danced in her brain to the same chaotic rhythm. She was determined, however, and through this blur of perpetual motion circling in her head she read, undaunted, through the night.

At the first light of dawn Frances closed the book. There was an enigmatic smile on her lips, her eyelids hooded, as if she'd spent a whole night of bliss. Something, *one* thing, had gotten through. She had understood that some truths could only be understood while drunk, in a state akin to stupor. She knew that this was all Nietzsche was trying to say, and with that she had the focus for her second book.

The Heisenbergs

Irma Heisenberg more or less hated her husband and he more or less loved her. Neither of them knew whether it was more or less, and so they lived an equivocal life, loving and hating in puzzled indistinction.

Oh well, she'd sigh, Who's to say love is like a perfectly vine-ripened strawberry—juicy, red, and sweet—with no mistaking it for a pickle? Who's to say it *isn't*, though, Irma mused, never having abandoned these romantic notions. She spent many an afternoon thus engaged in endless debate of this worthy topic. There is, after all, something between strawberries and pickles, she'd think; for instance, gooseberries; but Irma could not claim to understand the middle ground one bit more than the extremes. Twenty-two ambiguous years of marriage later, Irma was still pondering, still possibly loving when she thought she was hating, possibly being hated when she thought she was being loved.

Howard would be home soon. Irma patted her hair in front of the mirror and spritzed some cologne on her throat, just in case she loved him. She anticipated his arrival every night, and every night she was disappointed, for when he walked through the door Irma took one look at him and thought, Who is this man and why does he keep taking his pants off in my house? Whoever he was, he'd certainly gained a lot of weight and lost a lot of hair, neither of which had done much to clear up the question.

All these years she'd said nothing. What could she say? I may not love you? And what if she did? How could she tell? And now even the neighbors seemed to know something she didn't, but they wouldn't tell her. Sofie passed her on the street as she pondered these things leaving the bakery. She looked Irma up and down, inspecting her like a week-old carp, then walked on. Irma stopped and checked her underwear; her slip wasn't showing. Nothing was sticking out. Why was Sofie staring at her? The same with Pearl, who stopped to chat with her outside the bakery.

"Is something the matter, Pearl?" she asked.

"How's Howard?" Pearl inquired purposefully.

"Oh, he's the same. You know Howard," Irma said.

"No, I don't."

"What do you mean?"

"I mean, I don't know him like *you* know him. I don't know him *well*. I mean, how well do you really know anybody?" Pearl asked.

"Not very well."

"That's right. So how is he?"

"He's fine."

"Well, that's good news," Pearl said, almost relieved.

"Why?" Irma asked, suspecting that Pearl may have heard news to the contrary.

"What, I should be depressed that Howard's fine?" she asked.

"No, no, I just thought . . . never mind. He's fine, thank God. So how's Saul?" Irma asked.

"Saul's in the toilet."

"I'm sorry."

"*You're* sorry, what about me? I tell you, Irma, that man is a Bela Lugosi movie in an all-night theater."

"You're really that miserable?"

"Aren't you?"

"Why? Should I be?" Irma asked, again thinking perhaps Pearl knew something she didn't.

"Men, you know."

"Howard's a good man."

"And Saul is *not* a good man? Saul is a pearl," Pearl said. "Goodness has nothing to do with it."

"Well, I'm not miserable. I just can't say that I'm happy, that's all," Irma admitted.

"It's the same thing."

"It's not."

"Believe me, when you finally figure it out you'll be miserable. Well, a pleasure to see you as always, Irma," Pearl said with a smile.

Irma watched as her friend ambled on, her square behind shifting its whole weight from side to side as she walked. Was Pearl right? Was Irma miserable underneath her ambivalence? The very thought made Irma feel that she should divorce Howard now before she had the ugly truth staring her in the face. She'd hate to see her illusions destroyed, flimsy though they were. A well-timed divorce, before things got really bitter, could be as good as being widowed. She could hang onto the good feelings while there were still shreds of them left after the years of being mauled by the claws of doubt. Suddenly it occurred to her that if she could have anything she wanted in the whole world it would be to be a widow. It could solve the

entire dilemma of her existence. She'd be rid of
Howard; more important, she'd be rid of doubt. She'd
have more flowers than she knew what to do with, all
without the stigma and inconvenience of divorce. She
marveled at the brilliance of her idea. The only stum-
bling block was Howard's perfect health.

Howard arrived home that evening still in perfect
health and whistling as if to rub it in.

"I see you're home, safe and sound," Irma said,
checking him for traces of dyspnea or fatigue. "No
serious accidents on the freeway, I see," she said,
barely hiding her disappointment.

"Of course not," he said, pecking her perhaps lovingly, perhaps heedlessly on the cheek. "How you
worry about me," he said with a satisfied smile and a
definite look of affection.

Irma was not impressed. Perhaps he only felt affec-
tionate due to what he took to be her concern for his
well-being. If he'd known it was a death wish, would
he have been so adoring? These were the kinds of
questions that had occupied Irma's thoughts throughout the days, the years; and not one of these questions
had ever been answered to her complete satisfaction.

It was all different now. Now that she had considered widowhood it was as if a dark shroud had been

lifted from her shoulders. She felt so good that the idea of murdering her own husband was not half as disturbing as it might have been on an ordinary day. Anyway, she'd be doing it for love, for the preservation of what was, or might have been, love. And if anything was certain it was that anything was better than the dying of love of uncertain worth.

The Old Man

The door was jammed as usual and the old man had to push three times with all his weight before it opened. If he lost one more pound he'd never get in. He stumbled inside as the door gave way, and he sat down puffing in his blue plastic armchair. He held a mango in his hand. He looked at it and turned it over. It was perfect. He had never seen one so yellow. He had never eaten one. His tongue squirted. He set the mango down on the small formica table next to him, then pushed on the arms of the chair with both hands in a struggle to get up. He made his way to the kitchen, sighing and shaking his head.

The dishes piled in the sink made him wince at the thought of what Sarah would say if she saw them, but the guilt of this was nothing compared to the pain that she was dead. He banished her memory as he had done a thousand times and looked around for the mango. He'd left it in the living room and he walked back to get it.

He heard something scratching at the door. He stood still and listened but it had stopped, so he went to eat his mango.

The anticipation of ingesting such soft yellow flesh brought a circus to his mind, a blur of colors and naked women on horseback, elephants containing the whole of the African bush in their lumbering walks and ferocious lions who made his heart race. Oh God, what a mango—the first bite sliding on his tongue like a kiss. As he chewed he released its sweetness and stared at the kitchen wall. It was blank. He'd never put the pictures up when he'd moved. What for? The pictures were Sarah's. He should have buried them with her like the ancient Egyptians, but it just wasn't done. They were in the closet.

He looked out the window before he pulled the shade down, then he pulled the shade down and the day was over. What would he do all evening? Would the winds blow again tonight?

Sarah was a red scarf behind his eyes as he bathed, and then she was gone. His legs looked purple in the water, the retired veins floating to the surface of his skin. He grunted and stepped carefully from the tub, guiding himself as he would a small child. He wondered what he was protecting himself for. Today there was the mango; tomorrow, maybe a cherimoya.

The wind did blow, worse than last night. The branches of the white elm beat against the window like an anxious heart. Other than the scraping of the branches and the leaves and the wind, the house was silent. That was when Sarah liked to appear to plague him. In his mind they were happy where she danced within him like a twenty-year-old girl, throwing dandelions at him and laughing as she ran from him across the meadow. But she had killed the past and he couldn't forgive her.

The window had blown open now with the force of the wind, and he got up to close it. As he walked across the room Sarah walked with him down the aisle. She was all in white and her veil was blowing in the wind, away from her face. He put his arm around her to help her catch the veil, but she disappeared. She had tricked him again. Furious, he reached out and tried to strangle her, but she was already dead and he tumbled through empty space, falling to the ground and choking with rage.

He lay there. The night grew quiet. The white organza curtains blew softly through the open windows. Billowing up and rippling down, up and down, up and down, flying above his head. He watched them for a long time, mesmerized by the repetition. Now they were his wings, or were they hers? Or curtains?

When he awoke it was morning and the sun was warm on his face. He rubbed his head. His neck was crimped, his back stiff. He struggled to rise, planting both hands on the floor and raising himself up, butt first. He shook his head, mumbling something about gravity, and shuffled into the bathroom. He attacked his fatigue, his shame, with cold water and washed them away. Since Sarah was not making coffee he would have to do it. And he would eat the rest of the mango. It was a nice way to start a day.

The White River Scroll

Dr. Trainer knew he had found, in that dusty old piece of lamb hide, his dream. He had unearthed grants, international recognition, and, most important, a challenge worthy of his talent. He would devote himself totally to interpreting the primitive scroll—the White River Scroll, as it was called—for it was found in the caves of Syria near a dry river bed that was once the aorta of the ancient Near East. Now just white sand, it was referred to unofficially by nearby inhabitants as the White River.

The Scroll was written in an unknown language unlike any ever before encountered, surely predating Sanskrit or Sumerian by many thousands of years. No one yet had a clue how to approach the arcane alphabet of pictographs and abstract symbols, but if anyone could decipher it, William Trainer could. He had led the American Institute of Archaeology to its greatest achievements and was regarded by some to be the most highly gifted archaeologist alive, having deciphered thousands of scrolls, stela, and cave paintings around the globe. The now-aging scientist seemed to have developed an almost mystical connection with these obscure scratches and scribbles, which he turned into journeys through time.

Excitement ran high at the Institute in those first months, as Dr. Trainer and his team of assistants began to copy the peculiar "letters" of the message by hand onto archival paper. Their work, they knew, could open the door for the ghost of a distant past to enter their world. They compared pages, noting any repeating patterns or other curiosities, looking for whatever sense they could glean from the mysterious Scroll. They could glean nothing at first. It was not surprising—they all knew what they were up against. Nothing of such antiquity had ever before been encountered, let alone deciphered. At least the Rosetta Stone had provided the possibility of comparing known Greek letters with the theretofore intractable systems of Egyptian hieroglyphics. Though the Scroll was a total mystery, they took solace in the fact that it was ten thousand years old. Ten thousand years old! It was unthinkable that any form of written language had existed beyond a few thousand years before Christ. But there it was—officially dated and documented—a system of communication complex in organization, though recorded with the most primitive means. In Sanskrit-like wedge shapes, the columns of symbols appeared to have been dug into the raw hide with just the edge of a sharp stone.

After five years of fruitless study, frustration at the Institute mounted and the eight scholars assigned to the project fell to three. The interest of the public and the scientific community had long since waned, but after seven years it was revived briefly in the form of good-natured ribbing and some degree of less-good-natured scorn directed at the eminent Dr. Trainer. They renamed the Scroll Trainer's Blank Page in History, while his colleagues consoled him with the fact that his expectations had been far too high in the first place. No one could be expected to decipher such an ancient text. It was enough that he had found such a specimen, thereby contributing to the world new knowledge of the roots of language.

But William Trainer was undeterred, his curiosity and imagination aflame. Maybe there had once lived another race of men and women whose intelligence

matched or even surpassed our own; a species of intellectual beings who vanished like the dinosaurs, leaving
no trace of their mental evolution.

With so little to guide him, Trainer often found
himself musing over the Scroll for hours, and through
the years he had countless fantasies about its author.
For days it might be a man lamenting a brutal hunting expedition that left his small tribe dead; alone and
frightened, perhaps he had sought solace in this message to the universe. Holding the Scroll in his hands,
Trainer sensed a prehistoric despair that must have
been fermenting for centuries. It was a complicated
brew in his mind: bravery, hope, and infinite pathos.
How could he hear the message? What did it say? For
a while he imagined the author was a woman, pregnant perhaps and ready to give birth. Alone, she
waited for her man to return with food. No longer
agile enough to escape predators if need be, she sat in
the very cave in which Trainer had found the Scroll,
which had been remarkably well preserved in a niche
in the rocks lined with iron ore. She sat crouched in a
state of intense expectation and scratched out these
pictures. Faint and tiny symbols, barely visible at a
short distance, woven tightly together in a long, verti-
cal line like verse or Chinese characters. Maybe she

herself barely knew what they meant, but she was occupied nonetheless, those long daylight hours in the dark cave, in blind dictation from the primal mind.

These scenarios came and went with the fluidity of water, a continually shifting kaleidoscope of images. But for the last two years of Will Trainer's struggle to crack the intractable code, his mind had settled stubbornly on the image of a young woman, no more than a girl, really, who somehow found herself wandering the world alone. He had no idea what might have happened to her people, how she had come to be alone, or how she survived, but he was sure that there had never before been a woman on earth so alone.

At first it came like any of the other fantasies—came and went. But this one returned, and it returned again. And again and again, until finally it wouldn't leave. Slowly he became convinced that this young girl was the author of the White River Scroll, and over and over again he saw himself lifting her very life into his hands just as he had pried the Scroll carefully from the cave. She took on a reality in his mind—he called her Erana—and she was so tenacious in asserting her existence that Will Trainer had no choice but to let her live there. It didn't worry him at first, but after a while her presence seemed to challenge the reality of his everyday life. It was a gradual process, but inevitable perhaps. After fifty years occupied day and night with carved stones, how could he resist the fleshlike vision of a naked girl begging him for help? He alone could release her from the past, in which she had obviously fought so hard against being trapped. Her struggle was preserved on the dried lamb hide of the Scroll. As if it were her skin, Will sometimes caressed it as the sun went down, feeling its smooth, worn texture in an effort to know her mystery.

Will's wife noticed him becoming increasingly distracted, but there was nothing she could do. He hadn't even told her of his thoughts, for though they involved the ten-thousand-year-old remnants of a specter of uncertain gender, they seemed to him vaguely unfaithful. But that wasn't the only reason he had kept it to himself. Scientifically speaking there was nothing to tell, so he had told no one.

One day, perhaps in the unlikely hope of getting some encouragement, or to release himself from its grip, or maybe just because he was unable to keep it inside any longer, Trainer ventured his theory to his few remaining assistants. They probably would have thought him mad if they had taken him seriously, which they didn't. They reacted as he himself might have, if presented with a similarly wild hunch—they let it pass. But rather than bringing Trainer back to reality, their disregard only fueled his ardor. Now he *knew* he was the only one who could see her—it was his responsibility somehow to make her real. He could not abandon her to oblivion as if she'd never existed or had never been rescued from the cave. She seemed to inhabit him more strongly after that. He could see her eyes shining in his own when he looked in the mirror—a glow like that of stars that were long since dead in some distant sky but very much alive overhead. He could feel her breasts and the curve of her thigh, golden brown from constant exposure to the sun. And finally, in the endless silence of his thoughts, he began to hear her voice.

Her whisper was barely audible at first, just soft mutterings, but soon he could make out some words. Well, maybe not words exactly, sounds, but he knew they were words. There were all sorts of things he knew, things that could not be proven as he had been trained to do, but things that were in his mind incontrovertibly true.

"Winter," she said, "the frozen river of time," and "waiting to break into stars," "silver stars in the garden," and on and on like that, disjointed phrases. He could barely think straight sometimes. He called to her to explain what she was saying, but the lines of communication only seemed to go one way.

When it occurred to him that perhaps her words had come from the Scroll itself, Will became so obsessed with his task that he was unable to concentrate on anything else. Day and night he spent at the lab, carefully transposing the words he heard; he slept on the couch in his office, if he slept at all. Bleary-eyed and unshaven, the formerly meticulous scientist began to wear wrinkled, unwashed clothing that hung loosely from his diminishing, ill-fed frame. He had to know, and he pored over the Scroll, struggling to divine a code based on what had been provided by the voice. Or had it been intuition, or some strange force of knowledge from the morphogenetic field? The symbols swam before his eyes, barely visible as shapes anymore. The voice continued its flood of nonsense in his ears, but the pictures would not speak.

His assistants, who had dwindled down to two when the grant monies ran out, dwindled to one. While others ridiculed his obsession, Trainer's only disciple, a former student, remained loyal. Tom Franklin never stopped marveling at his mentor's dedication, his persistence in the face of such overwhelming failure. But now even he had begun to worry about Trainer's condition. There were rumors circulating that Trainer was losing his mind, and Dr. Franklin found it harder and harder publicly to defend his old teacher. Not that he had any intention of deserting him. The man was a great scientist; Franklin saw him as a sort of visionary, and though his powers seemed locked up now along with the mystery of the Scroll, Franklin had faith that they would prevail in the end.

But matters did not improve. The threats of divorce from Trainer's wife barely seemed to penetrate the cloud that had formed around him. Franklin could be in the same room with him but feel strangely alone; a coldness seemed to emanate from where Trainer was presumed to be. A man was dying before his eyes, being sucked into the vortex of a past so distant that he might at that very moment be breathing Paleolithic air. Of course, Trainer spoke to no one now of his ideas, not even Franklin. Not that there was anything to tell—Erana's existence seemed to have risen from the void.

"The eve of man," she whispered one morning to Trainer, who was sleeping hunched over his desk. "The eve of man." He awoke and sat up abruptly, knocking over last night's cold coffee. "What?" he called out. He had heard her mutter this before, but today it was so clear, as if she were sitting right there with him in the room. He felt a chill, as if she had touched him; he felt her take his hand. He listened into the high ceiling of the empty office, but she said no more. He listened, wild-eyed with wonder and attentive for another clue. He had to surmise he'd gone mad when he heard only the echoing silence of a public institution before hours. He must be mad—a thought he had had hundreds of times these past years—but he went on listening. Nothing. He rose and cleaned up the coffee, took a bite of a stale raspberry danish, then tossed the rest mindlessly into the trash. He felt he was being toyed with, used, and it made him angry—pointless rage, blaming Erana, whose existence was speculative at best but to whom he'd devoted his life for so long. Too long, he thought, the blood rising in his chest, heart beating out of control. He fell into his chair and leaned back, trying to calm himself, but his chest went on heaving, his face hot and red. He was afraid. How could he have let her drag him down into the deadness of the past? But then he heard it again.

"The eve of man." That was all. That was enough. His heart was light again, there was hope on his face as he leaned into the silence once more. The eve? The evening, the end of day. Was she saying it was all over for man, or just beginning? Was the world dying? Was *he* dying?

"No!" he cried out. "It isn't true! I am alive, I want to live. Get out, get out!"

Dr. Franklin had arrived and heard these cries in the hallway as he passed by. He opened the door to Trainer's office and saw him shouting, so it seemed, at no one. He tried to talk to him but Trainer ran wildly past, scattering papers all over the room, then running into the lab to the locked cabinet in which the Scroll was kept. He tore it from the shelf, shouting, "Leave me alone. Out of here! Out! I've had enough!"

"Will, please, what's going on? Let me help you."

"Out, I said! You can't help. You don't even know her, you lucky son of a bitch. She's tricky, seductive, watch out or she'll pull you down, too! Go, I tell you! Get out! And never come back."

"Who? Who are you talking about?"

"No, no, you're better off not knowing. Please leave. Trust me!"

The idea of trusting this maniac was ridiculous and Franklin continued to pursue him.

"The Scroll," Franklin said, trying to sound calm, "Give it to me."

"I am going to destroy it. It's the only way."

"You can't take your frustration out on the Scroll," his assistant stated gently but firmly. "You're exhausted now. I know you'll feel differently when you get some rest."

"You don't understand," Trainer said. "You don't know her. She'll never let me go."

"Who? Who are you talking about?"

"The woman. The one."

"What woman?"

"The one who wrote the Scroll."

The doctors came and sedated Trainer and took him to the hospital, where he slept all afternoon. Franklin had managed to wrest the Scroll from his hands before he could slash it with a pair of scissors. It didn't take long for news of Trainer's collapse to spread through the Institute. And when he came to, he hardly seemed to know a thing about the Scroll. No one was surprised. Seven, almost eight years of fruitless labor was enough to push any man past his limit. Still, it was sad, such a great man, such an accomplished career with the promise of even higher achievements, left abased and demoralized.

The Institute saw no reason to pursue work on the Scroll. They received a nice offer for it from the

Museum of Natural History, which they probably would have accepted if Franklin hadn't happened upon a stack of copious notes when cleaning out Trainer's desk. It really was rather mysterious. Why would Trainer have withheld so much of his effort from Franklin and the rest of the team? He pored hungrily over the notes, which were sketchy and not very illuminating. In fact, in their way they were almost as mysterious as the Scroll itself.

The notes were presented to the Institute early the next morning, where it was moved they be discarded as the meaningless scrawlings of a demented mind. Franklin felt compelled to uphold the honor of his mentor, and anyway, he found the notes somewhat provocative. Though he admitted that he couldn't begin to see their significance, he was successful in convincing the Institute to continue funding his work on the project with a new study specifically designed to examine William Trainer's secret notes. Franklin even managed to generate new public interest, though it was based partly on the negative publicity surrounding Trainer's ill fortune. It cast a romantic shadow on the Scroll, like the so-called curse of the Pharaohs—those inexplicable coincidental deaths of the archaeologists who had dug up the Egyptian tombs. What unseen power did the

Scroll have that had managed to bring down a man of William Trainer's stature and drive him insane? It caught the imagination of the people, and many renowned scientists, challenged by the danger and eager to confront superstition, voiced their support. Perhaps Will Trainer, now a shadowy, reclusive figure released to the care of his wife, had sacrificed his career and his productive life as a man, but his project was still alive.

At the center of Tom Franklin's concern was a fat loose-leaf notebook, a hodgepodge of pictures, doodles, and symbols copied from the Scroll, beside which Trainer had written "Erana," "river of time," and various other bits of nonsense. Toward the end of his notes was a recurring litany—"the eve of man"—that Trainer described as "the obvious thesis of the Scroll." Franklin meditated for hours on this phrase, much as Trainer had done. But how had Trainer found this phrase in the first place? What made anything so obvious to the old man? Franklin wished he could crawl into Trainer's brain, which at this point would have proved to be a desolate journey, for Trainer seemed to remember nothing of the work of those years. In truth, he seemed to remember almost nothing at all.

Franklin sat at Trainer's desk, now his own. "The eve of man"—it sounded slightly ominous. He felt a chill on his neck and wondered if it was what Trainer had felt—like a wind blowing through the ages. It had finally carried him away, unable to escape. "The eve of man, the eve of man"—he could feel the fervor in Trainer's notes. Franklin knew he had never had the kind of passion that the old man had. He himself was more objective—intelligent, hard-working, loyal—he had appreciated, even idolized Trainer's passion, it was what had made him great. But was it also what had undone him?

Progress was essentially nonexistent and once more the project faltered. The directors of the Institute had been meeting with curators from the Museum of Natural History, who wanted the Scroll for exhibition. The impenetrable White River Scroll, they said, would be a big draw for summer and for a public hungry for mystery. So much the better if no one knew what it meant—they would play up its antiquity and its inscrutability. The Institute was easily convinced of the wisdom of turning the Scroll over to the museum: At least it would finally be put to some use, they said, and of course, the museum's generous offer would help recoup the sizable losses of a decade.

In defense of Dr. Trainer's dream, and trying to save his job, Franklin pointed out the importance of unlocking the secret of the Scroll. In his professional opinion, cracking the code was merely a matter of time. There was hope, he argued, though he couldn't exactly back it up with fact.

When the Institute handed the Scroll over to the museum they withdrew any further funding for research. Surrounded by champagne and caviar, tuxedos and furs, the tattered piece of lamb hide was presented to the patrons in its shiny new glass case. Dr. Franklin went instead to visit Trainer who sat as usual in his den, his tartan blanket over his knees, staring empty-minded at the flames in the fireplace. On his face was a pensive look, which Franklin assumed was merely etched there from years of deep thought.

The Scroll drew the public as predicted, and the people passed by it as they did all the ancient tablets and faded frescoes. They stopped, momentarily fascinated to be so close to a breath from such a distant past, and then they moved on, letting it slip from their thoughts completely when they reentered the world or sat down to their sandwiches at lunch. Franklin tried to forget it, too, but the words kept coming back to him— "the eve of man," "the river of time," "in his throat a song of me," and on and on. The chaos of these thoughts seemed to be begging him for order, and he convinced himself that order was close at hand. He had no just cause to believe this, and he had become a pariah among his peers for his foolish refusal to work on anything except Trainer's absurd project.

Franklin continued to gain some degree of solace from proximity to his teacher, though Trainer still paid no attention as Franklin sat shuffling papers and poring over pages.

"What does this mean?" he asked one evening, as he often did. "Where did you get, 'time was female, smelled of birth'? Or 'the frozen river garden'?" Trainer was mute. "What about this?" Franklin persisted, "'woman melting into man'? What the hell does that mean?" Franklin was becoming agitated, but to no avail—Trainer appeared not to know what he was talking about or indeed that he was talking at all. They lapsed back into silence and Franklin let the pages drop to his lap. He rested his head back against the chair and closed his eyes, feeling the fire flickering through his eyelids, its warmth against his leg.

"The eve of man." It was the old man speaking, his tired voice cutting cleanly through the long silence. Franklin sat up and stared without speaking, as if afraid to disturb the dream. But it was no dream. "The eve of man," his teacher repeated.

"Yes, yes, that's right, 'the eve of man.' What about it, though, where did it come from, what does it mean?"

But Trainer had slipped right back into his hermetic silence; Franklin could see the doors closing. Still, he had spoken, he had remembered. "The eve of man," Franklin repeated, "the eve of man."

Trainer began to laugh. It bubbled up from deep in his belly, "Ha ha ha ha ha!"

"What?" Franklin asked, taken aback, fearing the old man had gone crazy. Maybe just alighting momentarily on the old thoughts had pushed him over the edge again, and he felt guilty for disturbing Trainer's oblivion.

"Ha ha ha ha ha ha ha!" his mentor roared, tears spilling from his eyes.

"Will, don't upset yourself. Here, calm down," Franklin said, laying a hand on his shoulder.

"The eve of man!" he said, chortling, the gleam in his eye resurrecting his gray face. "Ha ha ha ha!"

What the hell am I going to do with him now? Franklin wondered, but then, with a wink and a giggle in his voice, Trainer announced, "It's her name!"

"What? Who's name? What are you talking about?"

Trainer leaned forward, his eyes sparkling like a

mischievous boy about to tell his juiciest secret, and he whispered, "It's her name." He could hardly keep from laughing. Shifting in his chair, he beckoned Franklin closer with a crooked finger. "It's her name," he said once more, sounding more mad than ever. But his face was alive as he repeated, "It's her name, her name. Her name is Eve!"

He did not wait for a reaction. As if the weight of that thought and the effort of speaking it were too much for him, he fell back in his chair, dead.

Franklin tried to revive him but he was gone. Alarmed, he circled helplessly around the lifeless body like a loyal old dog, but then he stopped. He couldn't help smiling at the look on the old man's face: peaceful, and still sweet with the trace of laughter.

Eve, he thought. Was the eve of man the *Eve* of man? It was impossible, but that's what the old man seemed to be saying—that what he had found was Eve's diary, the Eve of Adam, the mother of mankind!

Of course it was preposterous. Maybe that was why he was laughing. Franklin had followed Trainer into some pretty dubious territory, but *this* . . . Eve? No one actually believed there had been such a person, and even if there had been, she surely would have existed long before 10,000 B.C. Preposterous. They were scientists. No one could ever accuse him of betraying the old man's vision, but he had to face facts—he had done all he could. He might as well accept it. Trainer was gone.

He'd barely had a week to mourn this loss when Trainer's wife presented Franklin with five final pages of her husband's notes. She had found them, she said, in the drawer of his nightstand. Unlike the barely legible chicken scratches he had scrawled in his notebook, these words were neatly written in Trainer's hand: *The Eve of Man.* Under it, laid out in the same form as the symbols of the Scroll, Trainer had written:

I was the garden
in which man was created,
I was the flowers
the fruit, the trees
the air he breathed.
Eve of man, I waited
to be created
while I created him,
and in and out
and in and out
are edges of the same surface
turning
when the river thaws.

I was the garden
the frozen river of time.

I was centuries
waiting
I was time
waiting
I was the stars
waiting to break into stars
and stars and stars and planets,
planets and planets, dark
and one planet
with a garden.

I was the garden,
the frozen river of time.

Time was female, smelled of birth.
I was the birth
into which he struggled dying,
and in and out
and in was out
each the other edge of the same surface
was time itself
turning.

I was the eve of man

and he was cold and dying
frozen in the river of time.

I was not God
he was not God
We were God
but We did not exist,
I was the breath he couldn't see,
he couldn't see the garden,
he couldn't see me.
I was the garden
in which he was
not, not knowing
that what is seen becomes visible
and what cannot be seen
is frozen in the river of time.

He was cold alone
and I was
and We were
frozen in the river of time;
and together we were
no one
waiting
to be.

He couldn't see the garden,

the trees, the green
he couldn't see
without seeing woman
is man is
each the other edge
of the same surface spinning

He couldn't see We were God
frozen in the Eve of man
who is I
in the morning
waiting to be born,
the frozen river
waiting to be
woman melting to be man,
to be born
woman in man.

In the ever winter river of time
he was this litany.
I was breathing
in his throat—
a song.
We were the song,
apple-sweet,
I was the Eve of man
sung in Adam's apple.

Frozen river garden
ready to be green,
to be seen and heard;
a song of invisible stars
finds where we are,
a shower of silver stars hurled like spears
penetrates the garden
and sizzles in the river of time.

No longer frozen,
bleeding blue and green
the whole garden is a river of time
and we, its mortal harvest.
I am not the river
I am not the garden
I am not I.
The garden is the song of woman
in man
a song which melts us into breath,
which holds us together
and lets us go.

He had done it. Somehow Trainer had done it, cracked the code, and soon poets and academics would be crawling out of the woodwork trying their hands at analyzing his translation. All the repetitive words and phrases corresponded to the repetition of symbols in the Scroll.

"What does it mean?" Dr. Eigner asked. The director of the Institute turned to the other two members of the board, who looked similarly perplexed.

"I'm not sure, but it's not the issue at this point," Franklin said excitedly.

"We are no closer to understanding anything about the Scroll than we were before," Eigner asserted. "Where is the proof? Where is the explanation of Dr. Trainer's method? Where is the evidence of any method whatsoever?"

"If you examine the Scroll you will see that the pattern of the translation is perfectly reproduced. I think you are missing the point here," Dr. Franklin said, trying to remain calm. "I don't know how he did it, but it is our responsibility to find out."

"You don't really believe this nonsense about Eve, do you?" Eigner asked with a smirk.

"Well, no, that is, I'm not sure exactly what I believe, to be honest. I know I have faith in Dr. Trainer's work, though. No matter what else it is, this is still a piece of writing that is ten thousand years old. We have a chance to understand something of the earliest human mind. Certainly you don't intend to squander that opportunity."

There was an awkward silence. The three board members shifted uncomfortably in their chairs and whispered among themselves while Franklin stared at them in disbelief. They looked back at him, thinking that another one of their own had been driven round the bend by this ungodly Scroll. Like the curse of Pharaoh's tombs, its mystery seemed protected from any who tried to enter.

Eigner cleared his throat. "The Institute deems it best for all involved to deny provisions for any further study on the White River Scroll. That is the decision of the board."

"What? Are you crazy?" Franklin shouted. "Don't you understand anything about what we have here?"

Franklin had to be escorted from the room pleading and cursing over his shoulder, clutching Trainer's notes. He was deposited outside, and once alone, he sat on the steps shaking, sweating, and gasping for breath. His brain was racing, boiling, his thoughts tumbled into each other, only half comprehensible. Maybe it wasn't Eve, he could certainly see that, but a sort of mythological seed from which the biblical story was derived. Was she part of an ancient literary tradition previously unknown, or was it just a fluke, a lone woman struggling with her own rudimentary